THE SONS OF TOBIAS

TOBIAS BOOK III

BOBBI BOLAND WHITE

WingSpan Press

Published in the United States and the United Kingdom
by WingSpan Press, Livermore, CA

The WingSpan name, logo and colophon are the trademarks of
WingSpan Publishing.

ISBN 978-1-59594-616-4 (pbk.)

First edition 2017

Printed in the United States of America

Library of Congress Control Number: 2017960017

www.wingspanpress.com

1 2 3 4 5 6 7 8 9 10

For those of you
who understand
the wordless depth,
Intelligence
and longing
in an animal's soul,

And for those of you
who are close,
very close
to discovering it.

CHAPTER 1

Bandit saw his sister go. He was almost half a mile away on one of the low hills west of his father's grave. They all had heard the gunshot – all four brothers coming to a sudden halt wherever they were, braking to a standstill in the cool air, their ears pointed, heads turning slowly towards the deathly stillness that followed the crack of the bullet's release.

For a moment none had moved – still as statues of bronze, their reddish coats soft, glistening from winter, their golden eyes like jewels, each one alert, each one knowing without knowing as the bullet struck, aware without allowing the awareness to be full, to render them helpless.

Then bolting suddenly, frightened, dissolving into the brown hills, the desert slopes, obeying the lesson their mother had taught them to run, to hide, to disappear as coyotes can do so well, melting into air, fading into earth and brush, hearts pounding, blood rushing – gone.

Until there was only one who stood his ground, who did not run. Bandit, moving as in a dream slowly toward the sound of the gunshot, not away from it, moving toward the

1

grave of his father where night after night his mother had lain keeping watch for Tobias, waiting for the miracle that was not to be, guarding the silent crumbling body while she sang for his spirit to return.

Bandit, knowing … knowing where the bullet had struck … moving … moving. And then he stopped, frozen as rock, up on the ridge above the desert floor as the minutes passed and one by one his brothers emerged, padding softly up behind him, standing together under the vast ivory sky of dawn, watching the scene unfold below.

He saw his sister. She was there, standing close to a young girl who was down on the ground trying but unable to stand, forced to her knees again and again, crawling slowly while his sister watched, crawling to his mother who lay in her blood on his father's grave.

The girl's thin arm was up and she was waving something small – a weapon, at a band of men who were watching her. They were taking hesitant steps toward her, toward his sister who stood trembling beside her, men with rifles, seeing his sister's terror, hoping to approach her while the death terror held her frozen – her body numbed, eyes locked, white as ice. What did they want from her? To kill her too? To rip her coat from her? To steal her thick and beautiful coat?

But then they stopped walking. They were fearful of the girl, of her weapon. She stood slowly, facing them, waving the weapon. And a terrible cry of grief went out from her, and the men backed up and turned away, acknowledging the power of that cry, unable to confront it.

Bandit studied the girl. Her hair was long and dark and she wore the shawl of the Shoshone. *Friend,* thought Bandit.

Shoshone are friends, protect my mother, protect my sister.
Shoshone stand proud against evil men.

Bandit took a few steps away from the rocks. He turned to catch the attention of his brothers. The men who sent death to their mother must not be feared; they must be punished. But this would be another day.

Now, he told them, eyes closed, bones rigid as he stood tall before them, now was a time for silence, for calm, for an affirmation that although their mother's life was ending in this world, she would be able to bless them from the next.

So the brothers stood close to one another, their shoulders touching. In this way they drew strength from each other. They could wait for their revenge. They knew that theirs was a power that would prevail even as it had prevailed for thousands of years. And the desert blessed these brothers of the empty land, the endless sky. And peace entered into them.

The four brothers were seven months old; they had left the den long ago, traveling at first with their mother and their sister, hunting and playing as a family, venturing off on their own only for a day or two but always returning to their mother's lair, proud to protect her, proud to protect their only sister. She was smaller and thinner than her brothers, shy and gentle, a shadow of her mother with the same golden eyes that their father, long-haired renegade canine protector, had loved so much, so desperately.

Bandit remained by his rock as one by one his brothers moved away. He watched the girl for a long time after the shot that had entered his mother and caused the slow expanding pool of blood beneath her. He studied the protective movements of the girl as she placed her shawl over the still body and reached out to comfort the slight trembling form of his sister.

The men had left, turning, retreating to their truck, kicking up dirt and sand as they sped off to the north. But then, down by the little chapel close to the road, another truck appeared and stopped, and after a few moments the girl began walking toward it.

Bandit watched his sister follow the girl, a few paces behind, wobbling on her long legs, closer and closer to the truck by the road.

A man from the truck went to the girl and embraced her. He walked out to the grave then, carrying a long shovel and Bandit understood what would be done.

The man buried Bandit's mother with reverence, leaving the protective shawl upon her, which was right and good. Until it was finished and the man walked back to the road, and Bandit knew sorrow for the first time in his life as he looked at the empty ground and the sad mound of earth beneath which his mother lay.

He thought of his sister then. Where would she go? She had clung to her mother, seeming too fragile to run with her brothers, unable to keep up with their bursts of speed, their twists and turns, the roughness with which they tested each other's strength. But all that must change now. They would teach her, encourage her, until she grew to be one of them.

Bandit sighed. He looked out toward the road. And then he looked again. She was gone. She had vanished. And the truck also was gone.

Bandit moved quickly down the hill and crept to the spot where the man from the truck had buried his mother. There he stopped, and he felt his soul drop once more, dropping into an endless well of darkness. And he knew that his mother would never return.

Bandit walked to the road. He walked to the spot where the truck tires had made an impression in the sand and he scented the area carefully. He did not need to scent the impressions left by the men who had killed his mother. He knew them, had seen their truck before.

They were hunters, scavenging the hills at dusk and if they had no luck they would wait all night, their voices loud and harsh, waiting for the first pre-light of dawn to savagely pull down whatever living creature they could find, hoping to discover and extinguish the secret graceful life of the few survivors left on this land.

These men were proud of their senseless kills, proud to steal the coats of the dead, strutting as they flung the bodies of their limp victims over their shoulders. Bandit had seen them do this; he had memorized their faces. They were killers who would return to kill again. They would be easy to find. They would be easy to punish.

But the truck that had taken his sister was not familiar. The route that it took was to the south and to the west, into unknown land that could be difficult to follow. But it *would* be followed.

And suddenly Bandit turned and ran. His was the speed of the wind, unmatched by any desert predator, 35 mph ...40 ...45 mph, a streak of fur over the desert floor and then up and up into the hills. He leapt, climbed in long stretches of sinew and bone. Until then – on the highest ledge, he looked south and west.

And he saw it; he saw the truck. Eyesight of the gods, clear and sharp, 15 miles, 20 miles – yes, he could see it! Master of earth's most desolate terrain, subject of myth and legend, shape shifter of the night, partner of the Creator at time's beginning, the only partner known by the Father for thousands of years – remembered.

Bandit's amber eyes narrowed and his neck arched and the fur on his back rose. No human, even the kindest, would be permitted to take his sister captive, would be permitted to take her from her brothers – to take her from her desert home. This he pledged. This he sang.

As the day passed and evening approached, Bandit remained high on the ledge above his mother's grave, above the long shadowed desert, the long road to the south. And through the desert hills to the mountains behind him, to the little chapel below and the small town to the east with its few lights just coming on, to the vast emptiness of land and trails that lay below him, Bandit sang.

And his song was heard. The hidden creatures of the night, emerging cautiously from their tunnels and dens, their caves and burrows, listened, and they heard. Then, one by one, Bandit's brothers answered his call. Long and low, they sang of their grief, a rising prayer that lifted their souls into the black sky, beyond the few stars, a prayer to be written beyond time, beyond change, firm and solid, fixed forever in the mind of their God, the God who had made them and sustained them. The God whom they knew had not forgotten them.

The Sons of Tobias would live on without fear. They would rely upon no one. They would succumb no one. They would trust only each other.

CHAPTER 2

The ride home had a rough start for Mira and her high-strung new friend secured with a simple slip knot on a long rope and lunging side to side in the open back of her dad's pick-up.

Jacob, who had been watching in the rear-view mirror and sensing the possibility of a sudden bolt for freedom, slowed and moved onto the road's shoulder. His solution was to make a bed of sorts for the pup. He climbed into the back of the truck and lifted her as gently as possible into the well of an oversized all-terrain tire that lay on its side in the corner.

The pup's nest was nine inches high all around with a sidewall "ledge" of six inches. Mira stuffed the tire with rags and towels, and pushed a small pillow into the center for cushioning. The reasoning was that once the pup got comfortable and felt safe, she'd settle down.

Maybe. But it was a job. No one wanted her to feel trapped, so there was lots of petting and talking with as little forcing as possible while Ben, Mira's younger brother, worked to arrange and fold the coyote's impossibly long legs under the rest of her.

She put up with it all. Until, finally, she was in. She shuddered a long sigh and checked out her chair (it was way too small to be a bed.) Admittedly, it was more secure than sliding around and bumping into things. It had been a trial getting in but it could be even more exhausting getting out, especially with Mira on one side and Ben on the other.

Not that she wasn't game to try, long legs splayed on the rubber sidewall, lunging, bouncing back, lunging again, until finally Mira just leaned in and hugged her, holding her in that awkward position for miles and miles under the blue sky, until finally she calmed.

She began to listen to Mira. She had never heard a voice so soft. There was, in the brief span of her life, only the deep rumbling in her mother's throat when the pups were new and tucked against her heart that held such tenderness. So as the truck rocked on and Mira held her with gentle words, The Jewel, because that was the name that Mira was giving her, abandoned her plan of escape and ended up half in, half out of the tire, her head on Mira's arm, her eyes closed.

"She's still trembling," Mira said in a half-whisper to Ben as he got up and reached to tap on the sliding window into the cab.

"I thought she was asleep." Ben leaned down to study the pup, "She's so much like Tobias but like a shadow of him … so small."

"I know," Mira slid her arm carefully from under The Jewel's head. "I think she's dreaming about what happened.

"Ben?" Mira looked up at her brother, "She shook so violently when her mother was killed. Her heart thumped so loud I could hear it."

"She's still not grown. Look at her." Ben sat down again, across from Mira. He was almost two years younger than his sister but already as tall, his voice deep, his dark eyes serious. He sat cross-legged as he talked, leaning his back against the side of the truck. "Maybe all animals feel that way when they lose their mother."

"Even little ones, ones that no one thinks about or pays attention to?"

"Sure," Ben glanced at The Jewel, then back at his sister, "Even us. Remember how it hurt when we realized that Mom was gone for good, that she was never coming back? Imagine how much worse it would have been if she had been killed. Imagine if we had to watch her being killed."

Mira didn't answer. "Ben," she said finally, watching him curiously, "I never agreed that mom was gone for good. That was you – remember? You used to say that I was stupid to believe that she'd come back."

Ben sighed. "It's been over two years, Mira. If she were being held against her will, her relatives would know. If she were killed, even accidently, don't you think they'd call us?" Ben turned away; his voice dropped. "Mom's fine. She doesn't want to come back."

Mira laid her head on the tire, next to The Jewel. "Anyway," she said quietly, "we thought Tobias was gone forever, but he came back, didn't he? He found us all the way in Nevada. And even when he was shot and dead and buried, he still remembered us. He trusted us to come and save his daughter." She looked over at Ben, whose eyes were half closed and whose face showed no response. "Well?" she said, after a moment, "didn't he?"

Ben nodded slightly. "Guess so," he said.

"See?" Mira spoke to the sleeping pup, "It was meant to be that we found you today." She sighed. "The desert's no place for a pup like you. You'll be so much better off with us."

Of course, not everyone would agree.

The ride across the desert and up into the forested hills took almost three hours. As the truck began to climb, The Jewel was awake, sitting bolt upright in her tire, too amazed by the scenery to do anything other than look, swiveling her head from side to side, her twin ears up, duplicating the mountain peaks in the distance.

They stopped at the new house. Ben jumped down from the truck and began to walk along the sweeping drive framed with pine trees that curved behind the house. "Come on," he called to Mira, " bring her this way, see if she likes it."

Mira approached leading Jewel. "Wow," she said quietly, "it's beautiful here." She moved up beside her brother.

The two teens walked slowly, surveying their future home. Lightening had struck it six months ago and although the roof was partially gone, a large blue tarp billowed over the opening. Aside from that no other damage could be seen.

At the end of the long driveway, where it curved into the yard, a small A-framed addition to the house stood, partially finished. Beneath its slanted roof, a rounded opening faced the woods.

Jacob joined the teens just as Mira stopped, gazing with admiration at the cottage-type structure. He slid her a look. "You can have that room if you like," he said. "I think I'll lay a circle of beveled glass in that opening, to let the forest light come in."

Mira was speechless as her imagination painted a picture of the room she might someday have. The Jewel, unnoticed, stayed close by, her rope trailing as she sniffed here and there in the grass.

"We'll have city water soon," Jacob announced, "but until then," he began leading the teens toward the massive ever-greens where the forest began, "we have this." He gestured towards a low rounded stone well. "Better yet," he continued, "… come on, follow me. Look!"

Down a slight grade of earth, lined with moss-covered rocks and lacey fern, a stream flashed briefly. Mira and Ben were transfixed. They both continued to the stream, Mira bending down and putting her hand into the water. The Jewel moved up beside Mira, stopped on the bank and stared at the water.

"Look, she's thinking about getting in!" Mira froze, "Nobody move."

The Jewel was truly in her own world. One step, then an-other, pulling out quickly as the muddy bottom alarmed her. She was not to be discouraged, however, carefully extending one paw onto a medium sized rock, testing it, then moving to another, the clear water running over her feet.

And then, suddenly, she was in, splashing and drinking and shaking sprays in rainbow arks of glittering droplets from which none of the humans escaped.

"She likes it – right?" This, coming from a wet but smiling Jacob, seemed so perfectly to understate Jewel's reaction that both of his children erupted in laughter.

The Jewel, caught up in the exhilaration of the moment and aware that she had now become part of a much bigger happiness that encompassed them all, jumped back onto land and crashed wet and grinning into Mira, bounded towards Ben, sideswiped him, and made for Jacob with a huge, irrepressible leap of joy.

It was decided that for the time being, Jewel would spend nights at the family cabin closer to town and weekdays, while the children were at school, with Jacob as he worked on completing their mountain home.

"Promise you won't leave her alone, Dad," They were on their way back to the truck.

Jacob smiled. "Don't worry, wherever I go, she goes." As they reached the truck he added, "As soon as you two are free for Easter break … when is it – two weeks?" they nodded, "you can spend the night here, camp out with her."

"Sounds cool," Ben moved to the back of the truck, lowering the tailgate. He called to Jacob. "Lots of interesting wildlife around here though – might spook her, especially at night. What do you think?"

Jacob, already settled in the cab, leaned out of his window. He cast a doubtful look at Jewel. "Well, I hope she doesn't spook easy. Anybody hear her bark?"

"No, but it would be better than howling." Mira giggled at the thought.

Ben crouched down beside the pup, and looked into her eyes. "Mira's right; you're a definite risk." He tried to scowl but the hint of a smile played across his face as he scooped the pup into Mira's waiting arms. "Look at this," he said to his sister, "a half-breed, no-good, crazy-ass hybrid. Kind of like us! Who knows what she might do?"

CHAPTER 3

It turned out that little Jewel was a champ about staying quiet, at least for the first few nights at the cabin. No barking. No yipping. Instead, all of her energy was spent dashing about, sliding around corners, leaping over chairs and onto beds, flying across rooms with her ears back and a maniacal grin on her face like a creature possessed (but seriously cuter.)

She wanted out – that much was obvious. When the doors wouldn't open in spite of her most frantic body-slamming message, she began to eye the windows, pacing up and down in front of the most accessible and then going back and forth on an invisible line perpendicular to the window, seeming to measure the distance she would need to tackle it at a dead run.

Strangely, as soon as anyone slipped the rope on her and opened a door, she was content to quiet down. Sometimes she was content to just sit in the doorway. Open space, lots of it to look at, to sniff, to consider, was all she seemed to need those first few days. Soon however, exhaustion would claim her, and after a big plate of food she would climb humbly onto Mira's bed and collapse onto her stomach for the night.

"Did you know that coyotes snore?" Mira was up early; the cabin's back door was open and Jewel was peacefully snoozing, her long rope secure around the small yard's only tree.

"No, guess I didn't," Jacob was slicing some bread for sandwiches while Mira stuffed the weekend's clothes into the washer on the porch.

"Will you take these out to dry before you leave?" she asked her father. "I'm so late and the next bus doesn't come until 7:30."

"Okay, I know. Here take this, eat it on the way," Jacob handed a sandwich to his daughter. "Ben's gone ahead; give him half if you catch up"

"Thanks, Dad," Mira reached for the sandwich with one hand and her backpack with the other. Suddenly she stopped, looking at Jewel.

"Go," Jacob said. "Just go. We'll be fine."

"Ok," Mira walked up to The Jewel and spoke softly. "I'll be back," she said. "You be good for Dad." And she walked away slowly, picturing the calmest scene she could imagine and talking to Jewel in her mind all the way to the street.

That evening, when Jacob pulled up to the cabin with Jewel sitting next to him in the cab, Mira walked out to meet them. She had charged her phone and held it up for a picture. *Good Girl*, she said without words to the pup. *Remember the treat I promised?*

No one thought it odd when Jewel, bounding down from the truck, headed straight for Mira and sat expectantly in front of her. Dogs often do this when they expect a treat. But Jewel wasn't a dog. And until that moment, she had never had a treat.

The next day, Jewel's second full day with Jacob, went well. Although he kept her on the long rope when various work crews were present, later in the day he let her free to roam the property, walking down to the creek with her, smiling at her antics as she trotted ahead with little bucks and leaps of anticipation while always pausing and turning with those big eyes of hers, to check on him.

That evening, home with the children, Jewel was more content than ever, alert when someone called her name and wagging her tail as she sat in the open doorway, watching the trees, studying the birds and tuning in to all the human noise and traffic around her.

Of course the arrangement couldn't last. Jacob was a habitat biologist whose job often took him overnight into remote areas of the San Joaquin hills and more recently, deep into the silent trail ends of the San Bernardino National Forest. So when his office in Redlands called with a new assignment, no one was surprised. He would leave early the next morning, check in at his office and be gone for the next 48 hours.

"What do you think?" he asked the children at supper. "I can take her with me; she'd probably be okay in the truck."

"That's crazy, Dad," Ben spoke up. "There are bears up there." He paused, his voice dropping, "She'd go berserk cooped up in the truck."

"It's forecast to rain," Mira was checking the weather on her phone. "Leave her here, Dad; look how good she's being!"

Jacob didn't answer, looking with speculation at Jewel's back framed in the doorway.

"It's not even for the whole day," Mira persisted. "It's

just until we get home from school." She looked to Ben for support, "Right?"

Ben nodded but had the same thoughtful look as his father.

"And if it does rain," Mira pushed on, "she'll be warm and safe in a familiar place." Mira paused. For a full twenty seconds she waited, looking from her father to Ben to her father again.

"So what if she breaks something?" she said finally.

But Mira had a plan. No way was she going to risk leaving Jewel home alone. Not with all those windows the pup had thoroughly studied, paced under, and mentally measured.

Mira hated deceiving her father, but the way she saw it she had no choice. It amazed her how much faith he put in her schooling when she, Mira, who actually attended the classes, was sure they were nothing but a waste of time.

Ben was just the opposite; school was fine with him. Of course, he was so good at sports he hardly thought of anything else. But that was okay; his fan club of adoring females happily took on many of his classroom assignments, and of course, most of his homework.

Mira sighed as she sat on the side of her bed the next morning, pulling on boots and tucking her jeans into them. Everyone liked Ben and everyone trusted him. Whenever Ben agreed with her, which he usually did, her Dad would feel he could go along safely.

Mira stood up, a slight thrill of anticipation in her stomach. She had it all worked out: she would go to school, hand in an excuse, and come right home again. But the question still nagged at her: why didn't her father trust her without first needing Ben's approval? "She's too much like her mother," he had said to Ben, "too unpredictable, might do anything."

"Hey, forget it," Ben had advised her. "It's just that you look so much like her. Don't stress; he'll get over it," and Ben had smiled his Ben smile. So Mira took his advise and she actually did forget it. Until now.

I'm glad I'm like mom, Mira was thinking as she kissed Jacob goodbye and left for the bus. *Isn't it good to be independent and to follow your instincts? At least I see things that other people aren't able to see.*

   Shouldn't I to do what I feel is right, Mira continued her ruminations, walking under the trees, *"even when no one understands? No one understood Mom either, or why she left us; no one trusted that she had a good reason. But I did. I still do. That's what trust really is – not needing a reason, not needing an elaborate explanation, just trusting because you know the person's heart.*

Mira arrived late to school, went into the office and handed the office manager a note she had written, forging Jacob's signature. "I have to leave after first period," she said simply. "Doctor's appointment; sorry it's last minute." She turned to go, "Oh, and I'll need a hall pass."

Smooth, she was thinking, slipping the hall pass into her pocket.

And it was. She was back on the bus heading home in less than an hour. *I bet you would understand me, Mom,* she thought, settling into the seat. *I'm not like other girls, but so what? I can speak to animals in my mind, can't I? And sometimes if I concentrate I know how they feel and what they're thinking. I know what Jewel thinks about – that's important, isn't it?*

Mira took a deep breath as she jumped down from the bus and began walking. Thunder rumbled across the sky. She shook her head as her long hair fell loose and free down her back. *I'm glad I ditched today*, she thought. *I'm tired of pretending I'm not as smart as Ben. When I am! I'm very smart!*

Mira hastened her steps. More thunder – a sharp crack and then another. The morning darkened. Mira looked up just as the rain began. Her heart skipped as lightening's eerie flash pointed a jagged finger toward the end of her street.

Sorry, Dad, she was thinking, *but Jewel needs me. She's scared. Right now.*

And Mira began to run. *She's real scared!*

It was like a dream – on the path to the house … on the steps … on the porch … drops of blood.

Mira stopped. The window was broken. The house was dark.

She knew it. The Jewel was gone.

CHAPTER 4

Bandit was feeling grumpy. Most people would think that a strong, aggressive coyote mix like Bandit would be able to heal quickly from the loss of his mother – the sight of her body in a pool of blood and then, moments later, put into the ground with only a sad mound of dirt to mark where she lay. They'd think the brave leader of a pack of coyotes could move on quickly from a scene like that. But they'd be wrong. Bandit was crushed, inside and out. And he was mad. He was mad at everything and everyone.

This sort of anger – the kind that came to Bandit's rescue the first few days after his mother's death, was real. And it was strong. It doesn't come to everyone who needs it, but its power is fierce when it does appear, standing next to the one who suffers just like the Archangel Michael, fending off the crush of weakness, assaulting that desperate sinking feeling, the pushing feeling on the earthling's legs that makes it hard for him to stand. Anger fights hard and true against these feelings. So, human or dog, coyote or cougar, we earthlings use it. We act tough. We act mean. We swear revenge.

And it can work! "Have you seen him?" Some of the

locals down at the coffee shop were quick to notice, "Mean as a snake, that one on the hill. Getting big now, not playful like he used to be."

"Got that right, Willie. Been slinkin around here for days. Looks evil," a second customer spoke up. "Wonder what happened to his brother, the smaller one."

A young man, sitting alone with a piece of Ella's blueberry pie, looked up and smiled flirtatiously at the shop's only waitress. "Ella here sneaks scraps out the back door to feed that little one, don't you Ella? Hey, Ella, you still do that?"

Ella turned away, smiling with her eyes. "He's doin no harm, that little one. His mother's dead now; let him have a chance to grow."

"Well, the big one's grown enough," Willie was determined to have his say. "Think I don't remember when he'd come snoopin round here, moving things from one place to another like it was a game? He'd take something, hide it, then while you were busy lookin for it he'd sneak behind your back and steal what he really wanted." Willie paused for effect, "Now here's my point. That scoundrel still got those same smarts, only this time he ain't playin."

"And he'd be laughing at us too – member that, Willie?" The second customer chimed in, "always had that grin on his face."

Willie shook his head. "Forget them days, Whitey. This here's a different animal, a thieving bandit with no joy in him. Got a rim of black growin round his eyes. Creepy. Howlin all night long. Needs to be shot."

"Howlin for a reason," the cook, a large quiet man in a white apron, looked up from the sink where he was rinsing out trays. "Saw his mother shot to death, shot dead and buried. That's his kin howlin with him. There's four of 'em; bet they all saw it."

"Bet they know who done it too." Willie squinted. "You don't believe me? Wait. That bandit on the hill is out for revenge; he's hella dangerous and if his brothers come to join him, them hunters better watch their tails." Willie paused, his voice dropping, "We better watch ours too."

At first Ella had no idea that Mira and Ben had taken one of the coyote pups. They had appeared at the coffee shop the day previous to the killing, right out of a late winter storm that had blown down half of the village signs. Looking for their lost dog, they told her – name of Tobias.

But the whole town, Ella included, knew that Tobias was buried 6 months ago, a stone with his name marking the spot at the town's edge. The children's story made about as much sense as the fact that they had come all this way on bikes, 50 miles on an empty road from nowhere to nowhere.

Even so, once their father had appeared, Ella had relaxed. The children were safe, and although she had advised them to consider adopting a new puppy, even recommending that they take in a homeless pup, maybe an orphan, Ella never expected they would confiscate a coyote pup from the wild.

The word confiscate is appropriate because Ella and most locals considered coyotes to be as much of a protected desert species as, say, a threatened plant, endemic to the area and not to be removed.

Also considered was the fact that within this particular corridor of land, running northwest through Death Valley and then into the mountains and canyons of some of Inyo

County's most treacherous terrain, coyotes were looked after and protected by the Shoshone. They ran with them, hunted with them, and played with their children. They belonged here. Even the half-breeds belonged here.

But now, strangely, as she heard about the recent killing and the repercussions it seemed to be having, Ella was rather relieved when the cook, whose name was Paul and who had actually witnessed the event as he watched unnoticed from the roof of his shop, told her he was sure that the children had taken one of the pups.

But which one?

"Well, I'm guessing it was a female – shy little thing, clinging like a shadow to her mother, saw the whole thing."

Paul poured himself a cup of coffee as he watched Willie and company leave for the day, still complaining about Bandit as they went out the door. He sat down now at the counter across from Ella who was absently sorting receipts.

"You sure?" Ella looked so troubled that the cook had to smile. She was a lovely woman, long hair the color of honey pulled back from her face, deep green eyes with flecks of gold and little rays of light emanating from her pupils, startling and beautiful to everyone but Ella who had no idea they existed. She seemed ready to explain herself but then stopped. "Are you? Are you sure?"

"No, but it makes sense. I don't think a male would voluntarily go with strangers." The cook leaned closer to Ella, trying to read her hesitation, "Why?"

Ella looked away. Although she trusted the cook to be a good man, she felt embarrassed to admit that she cared as much as she did about the little male coyote that had appeared at the shop's door each day. Ella wasn't married, had no children, and hadn't heard from her only brother in 10 years. It was a lonely life but having her little coyote friend made the loneliness easier.

Paul waited. He knew which pup she was worried about. As far as he could tell, no one had seen the little guy since the day his mother had been killed.

"Your pup is all right," he said gently. "It's probably for the best."

"What's for the best?" Ella turned to him defensively.

"That he lay low. It wasn't him that went off in the truck, Ella." And then, with a slow smile, "Don't worry. If trouble comes, he's ky-oht; he knows how to hide."

"I call him Francis," she said shyly, looking down at the receipts, "because he's friends with every creature; he just loves everyone." The cook watched Ella's face brighten. "Birds can sit right on his shoulder. The wild burros let him walk all around with them. Even the mice and the jacks have nothing to fear from Francis."

"Now wait a minute," The cook seemed incredulous. "Are you naming a coyote after Francis of Assisi?"

"I am," said Ella defiantly. "He's got the same magic. If a wolf came around, he'd go right out to meet him and make a friend of him." She paused then, deciding to be more honest. "But I worry because he's not pure coyote, you know; none of them are. He might not know how to defend himself if his magic didn't work. He's not as big or scary looking as his brothers."

Ella's eyes had begun to fill, so the cook looked away from her face and down at the counter out of respect. Her voice trembled. "He's very shy," she said. "A hungry cougar could eat him for dinner."

Paul stood. "No cougar's going to mess with him, Ella. Magic or not, coyotes born smart; it's in their blood." He turned to the swinging half-door leading to the shop's kitchen. "You take it easy now and have some faith. Your little one is doin fine. He just needs time to grieve."

They all did – but some would need more time to grieve than others.

Of the four that stood on the hill that day to watch their mother die, Bandit's most secretive brother was almost invisible. Rarely seen by anyone in town, he was a mystery, a ghost, an almost exact duplicate of Bandit that some would swear never existed.

Yet there he was: Buckshot, twin to Bandit in size and strength but with a slightly rougher, more grayish coat. His name, though few knew it, had been acquired when a spray of hunter buckshot pocked the right side of his face. He had been five months old and the pain had struck him by surprise, damaging his vision but not destroying it.

Buckshot stayed close to home after that, and closer than ever to his brothers while he waited for his eyesight to repair itself. Sometimes things blurred and he had to tip his head to clear them, but the end result was that his other senses sharpened and soon he left his mother's lair and stood tall with Bandit, using Bandit's eyes if that was what he had to do, in the grey light of dawn on the mountain ledges of their home.

Buckshot was admired by his family. He had plenty of soul. But deep inside he wasn't nearly as tough or as confident as he appeared. He was getting there slowly, but at barely seven months of age he wasn't quite there yet. The death of his mother struck him with a stunning blow.

After the killing, Buckshot retreated like a shadow to his mother's empty lair, deep in the mountain foothills bordering Badwater, tunneling into the narrow den where she had nursed him as a pup, hiding there day after day with his eyes closed, tail wrapped tightly over his face.

When dawn arrived on the third day he heard but did not respond to the familiar call of a young Shoshone man at the mouth of the den. This one had come before, always on horseback. He used only quiet weapons to hunt, and he had encouraged Buckshot to partner with him and travel by his side. Buckshot had begun to trust this man but now with his mother's death everything had changed. He, Buckshot, would give his trust, his friendship, to no human – ever again. Not even this one, the one named Kwinaa – The Eagle.

When, at twilight of the same day, Buckshot emerged to answer Bandit's call, Kwinaa was gone. A pheasant lay next to the den entrance, an arrow thru its heart. Buckshot carefully removed the arrow and took it down into his den. He picked up the bird and then, with the dead bird hanging from his mouth, began the long trot to his brother's side.

That night for the first time no cry but his, Buckshot's, answered Bandit's call. But two were enough. The hunters would only see one, one grey wolf-like figure barely distinguishable as it moved in and out of the darkness, a dusty phantom creeping out of the shadows, its eyes red and glittering, lusting to attack their human flesh. They would be disoriented, frightened, unable to find their weapons.

And so, as the moon's round eye watched without judgment, the brothers met, shared food and separated to close in upon their human victims from opposite sides of the black hill where the men had gathered to share their kills. Their rifles were already gone; Bandit had taken care of that.

CHAPTER 5

It was five days since the female coyote that had lain each night on the grave of Tobias had been shot, and two days since a wild wolf-like creature had come out of the hills to attack the hunters who had killed her.

One of the hunters had shot this creature, not with his rifle but with a pistol that he kept secured in a holster under his arm. In the confusion of that night his rifle, as well as those of the other men, had been moved, and in the dim glow of campfire the wolf-like creature had become two, splitting and then merging again in the ashen light, appearing and disappearing on both sides of the fire until finally a solid animal formed to attack one and then another of the startled hunters who scrambled in horror as they searched for their weapons.

"It was him all right," Billie sat at a round table just inside the door to the coffee shop, "it was that evil-eyed bandit coyote – that's who I shot." Billie looked down the counter, hoping to get the attention of two local patrons who were having coffee.

A few of Billie's friends, some with home-made crutches and large wrap-around bandages still showing the faded red of their bloody injuries, had followed him into coffee shop, sitting down heavily, complaining and grumbling as they tried to arrange themselves in the seats.

"Got him good too." Billie's eyes narrowed. "Tried to track him but couldn't do it in the dark." His voice raised, "Any damn service around here?"

Ella reached for her receipt book and came from behind the counter. "What'll you have?" She forced a brief smile and stopped next to the table, her heart pounding but determined to be polite. When no one answered, she took a risk, "How many coyotes did you see out there?" Ella's face showed no expression but her voice gave her away. Several of the men looked up at her in surprise.

"What you say, Shorty?" One of the men turned to his neighbor whose foot was wrapped in what appeared to be a homemade cast.

"Don't know, seemed like three or four. Maybe two."

"Hell no, it was all him," Billie spoke up, "Just seemed like more, son of a bitch is so fast." He was studying Ella as he spoke, "Gimme a steak," he said slowly, watching her hand shake slightly as she began to write. "He needs to die, sooner the better. Locals need to back us up," he paused, still watching Ella, "realize we're doin them a favor."

An older man, unshaven but with no injuries that could be seen, spoke in a low, harsh voice, "Well I say we go out there ourselves and kill all four of 'em. We're hunters; we don't need no back up." He paused. "The big one is injured like Billie says – makes it easy," he laughed a low sinister laugh, "so we find him first; finish him off – POW!"

The room was silent, everyone looking at the man who

spoke. After a moment he continued, "Then we find the others, hunt 'em down one by one, blow their ugly heads off, " he was drawing out the words as if he were enjoying himself, "…one …by… one … drop 'em in their tracks … strip off their coats and leave their flesh to rot … leave it for the birds to pick at," and he laughed again.

Ella was sick. Paul found her in the outside room that housed the toilet for employees. "I'll serve the food," he said quietly. He wanted to say more, offer to comfort her, let her lean on him. But he didn't know how exactly to do it. He had no experience with the physical side of comforting someone. He was afraid he'd do it wrong or give the wrong impression. So he left her there which, considering how nauseous she felt, was probably the best thing anyway. "Come back inside when you feel better," he said.

For the next few days, Ella was preoccupied. She hardly slept, spending early mornings before work, and early evenings after work, as well as all of Sunday, searching for Francis.

She lived in Tacopa, a village of hills less than twelve miles south of the shop, population: 150. It seemed to Ella, walking the winding dirt roads at dusk, looking into the yards she passed, stopping to talk to a neighbor or two, that Tacopa was just far enough from the violence for Francis to feel safe. She was embarrassed to tell anyone, even Paul, but sometimes at night she would stand out on her porch and in her mind call softly to the pup. Ella wasn't so sure about the power of telepathy, but she was very sure about the power of the heart.

* * *

"Maybe he'll find me at home," she mentioned casually to Paul. It was Monday morning, eight days since the killing, and still no sign of Francis at the shop. "He's very smart," she continued. "I think he's been to our village before."

Ella paused, glancing at the cook. "There's a Gooding Willow ... down by that little river we have. Coyotes use it sometimes ... for healing." She paused again, turning from his gaze, "It's like ... you know ... aspirin. "

"And you think Francis would go all the way down there alone?" Paul gave Ella a puzzled look. It was still early and they were busily opening for the business of the day. "It makes no sense, Ella. He's not the one who got shot."

"I guess you're right," Ella sighed. "He must have gone the other way to be with his brothers."

"Or he's still close by," Paul lit the stove and pulled out some breakfast supplies from the freezer. "He just might surprise us, Ella – come right to the door like he used to." Paul paused in his work and took a long look at Ella, "Feeling better today, eh?"

Ella nodded. "A little," she said, dropping her eyes.

It wasn't that Ella was crafty, or feeling devious that Monday morning. It wasn't that she didn't trust Paul. It was more a feeling that, although it was okay to hint at them, which was certainly what she was doing, certain secrets must be kept sacred and secure, no matter how much you'd like to share them.

Because Ella knew exactly where Francis was. He was hiding under her porch.

CHAPTER 6

Kwinn was worried about Buckshot. He had heard about the coyote rampage at the hunters' fire and he felt that Buckshot was probably involved. The following day he had found some tracks and followed them carefully. Two coyotes had traveled together. One was Buckshot; the other, unknown to Kwinn, was badly injured, his weight falling on three legs – not four, and traces of his blood appearing now and then along the rocky trail.

Finally Kwinn stopped. The tracks had disappeared. He looked around. There was no movement in the surrounding brush. He studied the barely visible trail that angled down a steep hill to the protected opening of the den where he had last found Buckshot. It was a good hide out. If they were there, they were safe.

Kwinn sighed. He had found Mira here the morning that Buckshot's mother was killed. She must have been following the coyote but lost her way, falling asleep as the sun rose. He had woken her, lifted her up before she could complain, and placed her just behind him on the tall mare he was riding, waiting until she had encircled his waist and he could feel her lean her head against his back. Then, without words, he had taken her through the hills to the small chapel and the simple grave where the mother coyote lay each night, and where he thought she would be safe.

Kwinn remembered Mira. She was slight with creamy, almond skin and huge dark eyes that held secrets he could only guess. It would be good to see her again. Perhaps he would be blessed with such a meeting in the future. But the universe must approve such meetings, Kwinn concluded, in its own time – not his.

Kwinn leaned to circle his horse. He would leave the brothers in peace, at least for now.

Two days later he returned, sliding from his mare and walking softly down the trail to the hidden den. He whistled for Buckshot and waited, watching for movement behind the two boulders that framed the opening to the den.

"Ah, there you are," he whispered, as Buckshot suddenly appeared between the rocks. But Buckshot didn't move, didn't approach him.

Kwinn waited. Catching a glimpse of Bandit's amber eyes in the heavy brush behind Buckshot, Kwinn put two and two together and slowly, in order not to cause alarm, crouched in the dirt to have a heart-to-heart with Buckshot. He did this silently, the way he usually spoke to animals. He closed his eyes, offered his deepest respect, and extended his good will with no conditions.

Buckshot's first attempts to growl faded to a rumble, then stopped. He also closed his eyes. After a long and silent space of time, Kwinn rose, slid back onto his horse, and left. That's all it took. Buckshot understood. This human would help the two brothers but only when they were ready to be helped; he would not interfere. He would not betray them.

But would this understanding extend through the weeks and months ahead? Did it mean that there was at least one human whom Buckshot could trust?

No, not yet. Instead, it would remain a question, a lingering possibility, a memory as sacred as the arrow he kept in the den; a moment of light between two beings, hope suspended like a pearl above the long and narrow canyon of a life, not falling, holding … holding.

CHAPTER 7

Mira was seriously ready to give up on school. This was the fifth day since Jewel had disappeared, and Mira was feeling so down, so despondent, she was almost ready to resign from life itself. Everything was wrong and getting worse by the minute.

She had already skipped three days and although the school had been unable to reach her father so far, it was a good bet that they'd reach him today.

Mira sighed. She sat on a low wall next to the bus stop, reading for the third time her neatly printed excuse with Jacob's forged signature. Should she hand it in and hope they would be satisfied? She remembered the suspicious look she had received when she turned in the last excuse. Oh, Brother, and here she was again. Considering how ballistic they would get if they learned the truth, maybe it wasn't worth the trouble.

Mira hated the drama. Jacob never yelled. Her mom had never yelled; "Hush," she would say, "if you yell the plants will die." Mira smiled, remembering her mother. *I need to be brave like mom,* she was thinking. *I need to be calm and just do my best.*

She had decided on a death excuse, one of the grandmothers whom she had never met – the one in Israel, her dad's mom. This grandma had sent her some cards and gifts and was always laughing when she talked to her on the phone; Mira was sure she wouldn't mind.

The death of a grandma in Israel seemed ideal because there was no way the school would try to verify it. The need for time off to grieve would be obvious and, of most importance, it would explain why Jacob should *not* be bothered.

Mira was saving the grandmother in Lebanon for another time. She felt less familiar with her mom's family. It seemed unfair to burden them with a death, even an imaginary one, considering the continuing political turmoil over there.

Mira worried non-stop about Lebanon; she had read about the bombing of an Orthodox Christian church (her mom's church) and the recent abduction of seven foreign visitors. Mira prayed daily about all this. She would never disrespect either of her grandmothers or their families; in fact she often wished she knew them better.

What did Ben have to say about her plan? Well, nothing. Whatever she did was fine with him. This show of confidence meant the world to Mira. When it came to brothers, she couldn't ask for a better one.

Mira knew that if the school discovered she had forged the notes, she would be suspended on the spot. But so what?

The only reason she was going to this much trouble lying and writing notes, was for her dad. Because *he* cared that she stay in school. Why did he care so much? She had no idea. It made life difficult just thinking about it.

The bus approached and stopped. Mira stood up.

Technically, she had only skipped two complete days – Thursday and Friday, because she had at least showed up for one period on Wednesday before returning home to find Jewel missing. She boarded the bus and sat down, swinging her backpack around to the floor in front of her.

Oh, Lord, she prayed silently, *help me. I'm trying. I'm really trying to be good. Please let them believe about my grandmother.* She leaned her head against the window. *And please,* she continued, *please bless and protect my Jewel.*

CHAPTER 8

We know that humans can sometimes feel, without words, when a person they love is in trouble – even across great distances. Possibly all intelligent creatures have this ability – why not?

Just like with humans, it probably depends on the depth of the bond, how much one of the creatures cares about the other, how sensitive he is – how often he stops and listens to the messages that come singing to him across the earth, or messages that appear without warning and drop like a stone into his heart. Messages that call to him: ... *Rufus* ... *Rufus* ... *help me.*

Yes, Jewel was in trouble and she was calling for Rufus, her reddish bronze amber-eyed, medium sized brother, the wise one, the Mage.

To humans, Rufus was a mystery. He was sitting so still when first he was noticed with the three life-sized Magi kings in the open snow-dusted stable on Christmas Eve, that everyone who stopped to say a prayer was sure he was part of the display.

He never moved. Families came up the hill, up the steps

in the soft light from the chapel's open doors. They greeted each other; they hugged each other. Father Bernardo stood just outside the pine-scented entrance and smiled at each one as they entered. "Look, Father," a child exclaimed, "the Magi have a dog with them. He's beautiful, Father."

But Father Bernardo didn't see Rufus just then. Only a few of the parishioners noticed him, whispering to one another in tones of awe, "It's a dingo, Melissa. Look, he came with the Magi. He's praying with them."

"I see. It's a holy sight, Papa. Maybe it's a miracle."

Father Bernardo was aware of the whispers, so after the service he went outside and stood reverently before the display. "Well, hello," he said quietly. And Rufus moved.

So that was how it began. Father Bernardo had a friend. And Rufus, not quite six months old, already without a father, and soon to lose more, had the same. The ruffing, rumbling puppy sound he made — a soft, questioning roof-ruff when the priest brought him some crackers and milk and sat beside him in the straw, was how his name was found. Other people could call him whatever they liked; to Father Bernardo, and to the little group of angels who guarded the snow-dusted stable, he was Rufus.

Everything about Rufus seemed secretive, almost other worldly. Some of the locals named him Magi, and believed that he, like the ancient kings, had heavenly powers. Others claimed he was just a lost pup guided to them by the stars, a good-looking retriever type that somehow came out reddish gold, and that could disappear and reappear at will.

Few guessed that his mother was the lone coyote female who kept guard at the grave of Tobias. After all, he didn't look like a coyote. He smiled and wagged his tail, and every other Sunday he was there to greet the children coming into Mass. Until that terrible Sunday when his mother was killed. And then he seemed to vanish for good.

But Rufus was still close by, burrowed in beneath the church, thinking. As deeply as his mother's death affected him, as deeply as it hurt him to recall it, it seemed to Rufus that she had agreed to such a possibility, had been preparing for it.

He remembered the day that his father was killed. The pups were small and had run to their mother for cover as a tall, seemingly out-of-control truck came careening toward them across the open desert. Tobias hadn't run. He had stood his ground, facing the enemy while his pups scrambled to safety.

Rufus sometimes wondered if his mother had seen the moment when Tobias' life was taken, when the truck blew his body apart and then swerved and returned to crush all that was left of him into the ground.

The pups, sheltered safely under their mother, could see nothing. But they heard it. Each of them heard it. And they knew.

Their mother had instructed the pups to stay huddled to-gether just as they were while she went down to inspect the body of their father. After a long time she returned without him and lay down with her pups and didn't move again until the following morning when the sun was high.

From that day forward Rufus watched his mother change. She began to withdraw from her pups, become more distant, more distracted.

Even when Tobias was buried and a stone laid over him,

she continued to spend more time alone, tolerating only his sister for company, growling at Rufus and his brothers if they tried to follow.

Each day she traveled farther away from them, returning only at night to lay on the stone of their father's grave where neither Rufus nor his brothers would dare to disturb her. Why? Was she waiting for Tobias to come back? Was she waiting to join him in the spirit world?

Rufus thought about things like this, worried over them. He was a handsome pup and he possessed many qualities – this is true. But basically, Rufus was a thinker.

With the coming of winter after his father's death, the long dreary days, the howling winds, Rufus was lonely. He felt rootless, out of place. His brothers were busy; they had each other for comfort, but Rufus had no one. Even his sister was unavailable and it was she who had been the friend he could count on. The nights were getting cold; soon he would need to find a safe place of his own.

So when December began and Rufus noticed the temporary stable by the chapel being built, he approached it with great interest. Day after day he lay unnoticed, in the dry grass high on the hill above the church, to study it. And as soon as the straw was laid, the statues brought in and the lights strung along the roof, he got up and claimed it for his own.

Was it worth waiting for? Absolutely. Whenever Rufus sat quietly among the Magi in the little stable, he felt a sense of peace, of protection. He could dream good dreams. But then one day in January, the lights came down and the stable was disassembled. So Rufus moved back onto the overlooking hill, and waited.

He knew that his mother's death was coming soon. Sometimes on the coldest nights, he would keep watch with her. She didn't hide; she lay in the open, under the pale moon, under a sky that was white with winter. He knew she was aware of the hunters, aware that they reveled in taking down an easy target – one that would welcome an end to her life.

So when it happened, Rufus simply accepted it. He burrowed under the church and closed down his mind and his body as much as possible in order to bear it. His mother, by her slow withdrawal, had equipped him to survive without her. He knew he could do this. But he was not at all certain how to manage if it were true that his only sister was also gone.

Since their birth she had been his friend. She had nudged him awake each day, groomed him, shared food with him, tumbled over him and under him, defended him, challenged her brothers if they dared to steal from him. She sang with him as the moon rose and slept next to him when the nights were cold. Rufus had lived on this earth for more than six long months, and the pup that Mira had taken was the truest friend he had ever had.

Rufus had no idea that it was the young girl with the Shoshone shawl who had taken his sister. Only Bandit knew this. But Rufus knew all that he needed to know. His sister was gone.

In the hours after his mother's death, into the evening and through most of the night, Rufus had searched for Jewel. He went into the hills and poked around; he tried a lonely song or two – just him alone on a flat grey rock a mile from his mother's grave. *Where are you,* he sang. It was a soft song.

Where are you? A listening song. But there was no answer. She was gone.

In the days that followed, Rufus stayed cold and numb under the church. He had no heart for fighting, no heart to join his brothers to punish the hunters. He heard Bandit's call the night of the attack, but he could not answer.

And then, on a bright Monday morning, eight days since his mother's death, in his mind, in his heart, he heard his sister call him. *Rufus.*

He jumped to his feet, came out from his den, shook his fur, his rump, his ears. Yes! He would find her. He would search the deserts and the mountains; he would travel all the earth until he found her. He had no idea which way to look, so he would look everywhere.

Rufus loped to the top of the hill above the chapel. He made his way across the open land, threaded through a long canyon and up into the mountain foothills. His mind was made up. Nothing would stop him.

Day after day Rufus searched for Jewel, mile after mile alone, blessed by the prayer of a single priest who watched him go, and by the whispers of children all the next week as they roamed the hills and searched with longing for the dog of the Magi.

Rufus began calling to his sister from the first night of his journey. He was going north where there was only rolling earth and empty endless sky to hear his call. It was a slow rising call, the call his mother had sung – high and clear, calling her pups to come to her. Each night, Rufus would call to Jewel. Every rising of the moon he would sing of his journey to find her. Until one night, he was certain, she would hear.

CHAPTER 9

On the evening of his journey's third day, Rufus was deep into Death Valley. He had traveled almost 75 miles from home when an angel messenger stopped him and nudged him to turn west.

That evening, the same evening that Rufus turned west, Bandit, who earlier that day had accepted a splint, two narrow planks of padded softwood wrapped tightly around his fractured leg, and some healing broth from Kwinn, was making his slow, deliberate way with Buckshot beside him down the road that led south from Shoshone. A purple dusk covered the hills and masked them in shadow. Their first stop would be Tacopa. Here they would call to Francis.

Ella knew. The minute she heard the call, she knew. She went to the door and opened it, the bowl of dinner she had just prepared for Francis still in her hand.

For many nights Ella would remember that moment – Francis creeping from under the safety of her porch and with a quick turn to look at her and a quick wag of his tail, loping happily to greet his brothers, licking their faces, prancing in circles as they licked him back, overjoyed that they had come for him.

She watched until they disappeared. Bandit was in the lead, his stiff leg invisible in the growing dark. She lost sight of them before they reached the two lane paved road going south, hoping they would turn north, or east, hoping they would turn anywhere but south. But Bandit knew that south was the way that the truck had gone. Ella knew it too. If ever a journey, a direction, had been pre-ordained, this was it.

But what about the brother who was not there? Bandit stopped. He had called to Rufus several times in the past week only to be met with silence. This was not good. Bandit crossed the paved road leading south and climbed a low mound of earth. He would call again and this time his brothers would join him. So great would be the power of their call that Rufus, wherever he was, would hear.

So, as the brothers watched, Bandit began his call – a long, low, rising call that would echo for miles across the land. Then, as the moon rose, an amazing harmony of tones emerged, each brother lifting his head, his throat, his soul, each tone separate and unique, an octave above or an octave below, rising and falling, peaking in a crescendo that reached high and then higher still, a song so pure, so intense that Ella, standing alone on her little porch, had to smile as she wiped her tears and turned slowly back inside, determined to do as the brothers were doing – to say her own prayer – for Francis first, but also for all who were lonely, or lost, or afraid.

So, by proxy, Rufus got an extra prayer that night, just when he needed it. Of course, Rufus had other prayers going for him too. Good thing. Two hundred and ninety five miles is a long way to go alone.

Rufus often had the uncanny feeling that Tobias was watching over him. Even when Father Bernardo left water and food in little dishes under the church, it was Tobias who got the credit; it was Tobias who, in Rufus mind, was the inspiration for every kindness.

As a pup of three months, Rufus was sure he was his father's favorite. Checking out his own appearance, he soon decided that he looked like Tobias too – almost exactly, long silken reddish coat, strong legs like his father's and soft petal-shaped ears that flopped over and itched him constantly, unlike his mother's stand alert ears.

Some mornings, Rufus was the first of the pups Tobias came for, even before Bandit. He would nudge Rufus to his feet and let him follow as he searched for breakfast.

Tobias taught him many secrets in those first few months of life, like how to look up to the sky and follow the red winged hawk to find food, and how to trail a scurrying badger to the bushy den of a potential meal, and watch as the dirt flew up in a spray as the badger dug. He showed Rufus how to slink even closer and to wait at the opposite side the bush until the mouse or gopher that the badger was hunting suddenly popped up his escape hatch, right at the feet of Tobias and Rufus.

Then they would try the trick themselves, Tobias on one side of the bush, noisily digging while Rufus crept around to the other side waiting for the little escape artist to appear.

Soon all the brothers understood this game. Even their sister learned to play it and often surprised them by discovering an alternate opening under a neighboring bush. She would wait there by herself as her bothers dug elsewhere, then bark at them with wagging tail just as the unsuspecting rodent dug out to look at her in shock.

Lessons like these were tucked in the heart, and Rufus knew he was not alone in his loneliness. He was sure that his brothers had heard his call and were on their way to join him, but he couldn't wait. He must continue alone, bravely skirting the territories of other wildlife families, his bronze coat blending into the red sky of sunset and turning golden in the golden sky of dawn.

Rufus traveled sixty miles of treacherous mountainous terrain in the next three days, going west. The hidden springs and wildlife dens in the many canyons to his south were now too difficult to reach; the mountains rose sharp and forbidding around him. There were no roads here and few trails, and when several spring storms flooded his path with moving mud, he climbed to higher ground, searched for a cave and buried his head into his fur.

Each night he would emerge from his shelter and call to his brothers, a call by which he believed they could hear his distress. So strong was the bond between them that Rufus never doubted his brothers were following. If he didn't hear their answering calls, he wasn't overly concerned. They were his brothers – they would find him.

And they certainly would have found him. The problem was that the distance between the three going south and their missing brother going first north, then west, kept growing. They called. They sang. They listened intently. But only silence answered them.

Bandit was the first to figure it out. Rufus had gone off on his own, probably north into the mountains, (not very smart, but that was Rufus for you.) Sooner or later the difficulty of survival in those mountains would turn him back. Once home he could easily pick up his brothers' trail. He could follow, or not – the choice was his.

Bandit wasn't cold-hearted; he cared as much about Rufus as the others. But Bandit was a realist, not a mystic. With both parents gone, he was the undisputed pack leader. He was the largest of the pups, yes, but at only seven months of age, he was still learning himself. And he was serious – serious about not wasting time, serious about conducting this journey safely, serious about finding his missing sister.

So while the others relied upon Bandit, Bandit relied upon detail. His senses were keen. And yet as sharp as his tracking skills might be, and as clear as his memory of the white pick-up that had etched itself like cut glass into his mind, it was the common sense of his mother that won the day. He must remember to always be alert for enemies; he must not allow the eyes of other predators, human or animal, to follow his movements, to predict his path.

And so, always keeping the road in view, Bandit moved his brothers inland just enough to use the cover of the desert scrub, the shadowed indentations of abandoned trails and riverbeds where they would not be seen.

He limped before them in the grey light of dawn, rested unseen with them in the glare of noon, and then urged them forward again, into the haze of evening – a strange trio of ghosts, barely visible within the protecting veils of night.

Bandit had a job to do – a job that took all of his

intelligence, all of his courage, all of his heart. Rufus, he decided, would be all right. Wouldn't he?

Well, maybe.

As dusk fell on the sixth day of his journey, Rufus stood high on a ridge that overlooked seventy miles of barren land to his south. Clouds filled his eyes.

He had passed well below Panamint Springs and was following a rarely used trail that led to a shadowed canyon that scented of greenery and water to his west. But then he had stopped. Something was telling him to revise his plans. Perhaps he should be heading south.

But why? All was empty heading south, just desolate hills one after another. Except, this morning as he had threaded his way through the cramped and pencil-thin crossing between two of windiest mountain peaks of his journey and emerged with relief onto lower ground, ... hadn't he passed, what was it? Not a trail but an actual road, one narrow road – empty and muddy but showing the tread marks of tires that had gone that way before. One road. Going South. Should he go back to it?

Rufus' eyes closed. It was sunset. Telescope Peak rose in dark shadows to his distant east where the canyon trails that he had crossed this morning had been wild with tumbling rock and rushing water. He could not go back that far, even if he wanted to – which he did not. He sighed. He was hungry.

Rufus wasn't sure which way to go; he didn't know what in the world to do.

So after a few more minutes on the high ledge, he sat down. And then he called. He called to his brothers. He called to his sister. He called to Tobias and to the father of Tobias.

He called to the One Who Watches, the One who would un-derstand his foolishness and his mistakes. He called to the spirit of his dead mother.

Rufus was ready to accept the truth. He bowed his head. He was lost to everyone and everything. No one could hear him. He was alone.

And then he knew. He understood. He opened his eyes. A great weight seemed to lift from his shoulders and he breathed long and deep. Once more he looked south but now the clouds were gone – his vision was clear.

Desolate or not, this was the way. If it took many dry and torturous miles, many more hours of hunger and of barren, unfamiliar terrain until the final stretch of land that would lead him to the forest where Jewel lay, he was up to it. Tobias was watching. And he, Rufus, had finally been heard.

Rufus was immensely grateful. He never questioned how or why his journey had been recognized, and blessed. But he was certain that it was.

CHAPTER 10

That night, the night that Rufus' journey was blessed, he paused briefly just before midnight to dig a shelter for a few hours sleep. He was traveling south with new energy, running parallel to the peaks of the Panamint Range to his west, not tempted to veer from his path as he covered the miles in record time. Finally he slept.

When Rufus awoke, refreshed and filled with trust that the way before him had been approved, he was still 85 miles due north of that final stretch of desert leading to the forest that was holding Jewel.

Mira, on the other hand, was only thirty-five miles from the diabolical snare in which Jewel was struggling as the braided cable of the trap pressed tightly around her young body. Those thirty-five miles however were steep. The few trails used by antelope and deer were thick and overgrown. Narrow canyons sliced unexpectedly between forested hills, knifing black and forbidding as they cut this way and that, invisible from above and hiding treacherous pools of sunless water far below.

So while Rufus' path through the brown hills and into the wide desert beyond, although farther, was clear and open, Mira had no path at all.

Not that a small problem like that was going to stop Mira.

"Dad, Jewel is in trouble; I feel it. I think she's trapped somewhere."

"Never mind." Jacob was working on his truck in the early light. It was Wednesday morning. He glanced at his daughter. "Just go to school, Mira. One more day; that's all I ask."

"That's all you can say?" Mira felt a mixture of shock and dismay. "Never mind, is all you can say?"

Jacob straightened. He looked directly at Mira and sighed deeply, "You need to be patient, Mira." He paused, glancing aside as he talked. "Tomorrow, we'll go up to the new house." He glanced at her quickly, then looked away, "We'll have better chance of finding her by starting there."

Mira studied her father, "Why? Did someone see her?"

"I'm not sure." Jacob looked back at Mira, his eyes serious. "Someone may have seen her in the woods close to our house. It's possible." He turned back to his work, "Go on, now. We'll talk tonight."

Mira turned, unable to speak, and began jogging for the bus. Her heart was racing; maybe Jewel was safe!

Mira slowed to a walk. It was a great relief to hear that Jewel may have been sighted but the news had come with a warning that had nothing to do with Jewel.

The "we'll talk tonight" was what worried Mira. *Talk about what?*

Mira slumped in her seat on the bus. When she had

forged Jacob's signature, skipped school and turned in her elaborate excuses, she had felt justified. After all, who was she hurting? Jacob didn't know anything about it; possibly he'd never know.

But now, recalling the look he had given her when he mentioned school, Mira realized the truth. Somehow he did know. Yes, she was sure of it; he definitely knew.

He'll probably never trust me again, she was thinking. *He probably hates me.*

But Jacob could never bring himself to hate his daughter. Yes, he knew all about the forged notes and the missed school days searching for Jewel. And someday he would explain to her that what she had done was more serious than she probably realized. But for now he had other priorities. The sighting of Jewel was no guarantee but the chance to bring her home would have to come first.

So the "talk" that Mira dreaded never occurred. Well, it actually did occur about three years later, both of them doubling up in laughter as they sat by the fireplace in the new house with Jewel at their feet and Jacob describing the sympathy cards, the announcement of a special service in the school chapel, and the Most Sincere Condolences calls he had received from the principal and staff at Mira's school – all for his very-much-alive mother.

Mira admitted how guilty she had felt, and how difficult it had been to even look at him once she realized that he knew. She never lied to him again, she told him softly, although sometimes (and this part made him smile) it wasn't easy.

If there was such a thing as a perfect father, Mira would tell him, closing the conversation shyly, head down, eyes almost closed, she and Ben had been given one. They hadn't earned it; they certainly didn't deserve it; but there it was – a gift. And a lifetime, she would tell him with tears in her eyes, wasn't long enough to say thank you.

They arrived at the new house by mid-morning the next day, the pick-up packed with supplies. Jacob had been called on another job so after getting things settled he was anxious to bring Mira and Ben down the road to meet their neighbors who had been told about Jewel and who had offered to help while he was gone.

"They might have a surprise for you," he told the children, walking down the road with them in early afternoon, sunlight splashing in bright patterns around them, the neighbors' red roof just visible through the trees. "No, not Jewel; something else," he had answered their anxious looks with a sly smile, refusing to say another word.

Mira was barely able to keep from running. Maybe it was a lead, a direction in which to begin their search, or a map to help them navigate the unfamiliar trails. Or maybe it was something big – mentors, actual guides – guides who understood the dangers of the wandering of forest paths, guides who could be counted on to keep them safe.

Well, in a way, yes. Yes! Horses!

Two beautiful, intelligent horses that had traveled the backwoods, the mountains and canyons of this land for almost ten years. Horses that could neither be spooked by encounters with wildlife, nor be persuaded to enter a deceptively tranquil stream that could morph in minutes into a torrent of water, a trap for even the most sure-footed of animals.

No human guides were needed. No map. "Just loose the

reins," they were told, lay them on their necks and bend close to them and whisper, *"Home ... take me home."*

Which they did, more than once when they had lost the trail and darkness was about to catch them.

So although they didn't find their little Jewel those first few days, and although they were sore to the bone and scraped by many a tree branch and many a spray of thorny brush, they were learning the hills, and they were getting closer.

CHAPTER 11

Kwinn knew that Bandit's pain was getting worse.

Several days after his silent communication with Buckshot, he had approached the den once more, sitting comfortably on the ground as he put together a temporary splint for Bandit's leg.

The canines, of course, knew that he was there, sitting right in front of their hideaway, and not going anywhere. Curiosity finally got the better of them, as Kwinn had guessed it would, and they emerged, one at a time – first to observe him from a respectful distance, and then to approach with caution for a sniff or two.

But winning Bandit's trust took many hours. Not until he lay on his stomach next to Kwinn's supplies and reached for a taste of the dried meat that Kwinn was offering, was the deal done.

The splint, however, was far from perfect. Kwinn did his best to strap it on securely, but with Buckshot pacing nervously and practicing little snapping noises whenever Bandit twitched or seemed to signal that he'd had enough, Kwinn had serious doubts that the splint would last.

By returning the following morning, he had hoped he could do more. But they were gone – both of them, Buckshot and Bandit.

Kwinn rode slowly as he tracked them through the hills, past the grave of Tobias and over the salt flats to Tacopa. Where were they going? What could possibly be so important?

The tracks stopped thirty yards from a small frame house. Here they were joined by another set of tracks – a joyous greeting, much dancing about in the dust. Ah, a recent reunion.

Kwinn sat quietly on Molly and studied the house. He watched as Ella came out on her porch. He waved once, lifting his arm high, pausing until she saw him, and then turning to follow the three sets of tracks as they headed out across the wide desert west of Tacopa.

Ella stood quietly in the early light watching Kwinn. She wasn't sure who he was, but she was sure he was Shoshone. So, she concluded, if he were following the tracks of Francis and his brothers, it was not to worry. Shoshone would never harm their desert friends.

As the morning progressed, Kwinn's concern for Bandit deepened. The tracks he was following showed a ragged but steady gait, a three-legged trot, a slow, uneven lope. This would be murder on Bandit if it continued. His leg, if not securely braced – not with a mere splint but with a real cast, could end up a jagged almost useless appendage an inch or two shorter than the rest.

Bandit, the strong and magnificent pack leader, would be a cripple.

By mid-afternoon Kwinn was able to pick up his pace.

Although still trailing the brothers by about eight hours, he knew that he was gaining ground. He had lost the tracks several times that morning as they veered inland, but with close inspection he would find them again, emerging from a thick clump of brush, or if the tracks belonged to Buckshot, veering off to investigate some oddly placed piles of shale.

He paused once, his curiosity aroused when he discovered where Buckshot had scrounged for food – his characteristic scratches still fresh under a cluster of desert sage. Kwinn studied the ground beneath the largest bush; he checked around several smaller bushes close by. No sign of a creature's escape, no sign of a hasty meal – just frustrated circles. Then, with Bandit leading, they were off again, single file, direct and steady. But to where?

As twilight approached, Kwinn stopped to rest where the brothers had rested the night before – arriving late, probably well after midnight. Bandit had found a spot behind a string of seemingly deserted mobile homes at the end of a narrow overgrown trail, where two buckets of water from an ancient well had been generously left for whoever might pass.

Kwinn dismounted. "We're only about six hours behind them now." he spoke to Molly as she noisily drank and he searched through his few supplies for something to eat. "Tomorrow we find them."

As the desert night encompassed them, Kwinn pumped the well to refill the buckets while Molly, almost invisible in the complete darkness, chomped on some tall rabbitbrush nearby and seemed to sigh with contentment.

"Come on, Girl," Kwinn moved silently behind the trailers and then a short distance more into a grove of cottonwood trees with Molly behind him. "They would have felt safest back here," he said softly, stopping, not bothering to look for proof, sensing their recent presence all about him in the air.

The moon, low against the horizon and barely visible behind wisps of cloud that trailed like ghosts across the sky, gave only the palest light through the trees. Kwinn knelt to study the small bed that Buckshot and Francis had made, pushed halfway into a mound of dirt for protection, a space for each of them to curl up with Bandit in the middle.

Bandit whose exhaustion must have been too great to do anything but collapse and work on loosening his splint, made the biggest mess, leaving behind a few scraps of bloody cloth, a shred of gauze, and a record of frustration and pain that ate at Kwinn's heart in a way that drew long lines down the sides of his face and closed a grey pall of sadness over his eyes.

CHAPTER 12

Kwinn and Molly were up before dawn, refreshed and eager to begin the day, hopeful the brothers would suddenly appear, materialize on the trail ahead, regal and perfect, like statues of bronze on the desert floor.

First light found them loping along with all that impossible hope in their hearts as a hint of ivory appeared in the sky, the highway a thin and distant ribbon to their south, and the soft feel of a desert breeze brushing their skin. It was a beautiful morning with the smell of sage and juniper in the air, a boundless and familiar cathedral in which to trust that all would be well.

But things began slowly to slide as the morning wore on with no sight of Bandit, no sight of Buckshot or Francis, only the tracks fading and endless. Doubt began to press upon them, a growing sense of uncertainty, of apprehension. Kwinn fought it, dismissed it. But the image of his failure to find Bandit alive continued to fight back, slipping its long fingers into his thoughts, chilling them.

By midmorning the sky had turned a somber grey, heavy with clouds, and by noon the world had dimmed and darkened and the tracks were lost completely. Molly slowed her pace.

Kwinn dismounted. Molly had found the bright green pad of a succulent cactus, new and spineless, and he smiled as he watched her shake her head in anticipation of the challenging treat, her skin quivering and her tail swishing in the still air. Molly was right. It was time for a rest.

Kwinn sat down on the desert floor and checked his supplies: the healing salve, the double roll of gauze, the little sack of gypsite he had mined from the dry shelf of an ancient salt lake close to home. The fine powder of gypsite would need only water to soften and spread, sinking into the gauze and then hardening quickly into a cast. The gypsite was harmless; Bandit could chew on it all he liked.

Kwinn shifted his position uneasily. He sensed the impending futility of his plan but pushed it away. It was a rocky situation but not a hopeless one.

Kwinn and Molly resumed their journey into a slate grey day that smelled of rain. As the brothers' tracks became visible again, the sad dragging of Bandit's leg appeared leading the others to a shallow drink of water from a muddy depression at the edge of an isolated wash. How close were they now – four hours? Three?

Kwinn grimaced. He knew that Bandit's exhaustion would soon take its toll. The pain in his leg would soar through his bones with a commanding force that even Bandit could not overcome, driving him down and holding him there, helpless on the desert floor.

But no – not helpless! The tracks were still visible; Kwinn and Molly would find him. With some crushed aspirin from Kwinn's hand, some dried meat and a cool drink of water, Bandit would allow the splint to come off completely. A numbing salve could then be applied and fresh gauze wrapped tightly around his throbbing leg.

The plaster cast of natural gypsum, smoothed by Kwinn's own hand, would harden while they rested and Bandit was finally free from pain.

Nice dream. But it never happened.

Because when Kwinn arrived at the spot where Bandit had lain two hours before, no one was there but a distraught Buckshot, circling round and round a bloody mess on the desert floor where skidding tire marks had gouged wide tracks before they disappeared beneath a storm filled western sky – a sky which, as they watched, was lowering and slanting towards them with fine needles of rain that stung like ice in the growing dark.

Buckshot lifted his head. He turned slowly. His bad eye hurt him so he lowered his head to press it for a few moments against his leg. Then he straightened.

Things were bad, really bad; he knew it and Kwinn, gazing numbly at the shadowed desert wash, the depression of dried mud where Bandit's futile struggle had occurred, also knew it and could read the force of that struggle, could read the implications of it.

Buckshot lowered his head; he should have seen it coming. Twice that morning Bandit had stumbled, almost fallen. He had pulled himself up each time, but the fierce determination with which he had led them until today was gone, drained from his eyes, leaving him slumped and empty. Then, he had stopped – just stopped. What was going on?

Francis and Buckshot had watched in amazement as Bandit made camp right where they stood – right there in the open, on the wide and deeply rutted path of an arid riverbed at three o'clock in the afternoon. There was no cover, nothing to eat. Although empty now, the trail showed signs of use by other animals, occasional trucks and recreational vehicles all of which could reappear at any time to claim the trail, never suspecting that Bandit's body lay in their path. Worst of all, rain was threatening; the wash would fill quickly with water and debris. But if Bandit realized any of this, he didn't care. He hurt too much to care. And so he finally sank down to rest. His eyes closed.

Buckshot had begun to pace exactly as he was doing now with Kwinn and Molly watching him. Pacing was his habit when things got bad, when confusion set in, when his eye hurt and his vision began to blur.

Kwinn recognized this. He knew Buckshot's fears and how he had learned to deal with them. But he also knew the fierceness of Buckshot's pride, so he looked away.

Kwinn dismounted. He turned from Buckshot and carefully surveyed the scene. He could tell where Bandit had lain at first, on the side of the trail. But this was not where the blood was. The bloody mess was a few yards away as if Bandit had struggled to get up and moved down the wash before ....

Kwinn looked up. Buckshot had stopped pacing. He looked across the trail into Kwinn's eyes. A low rumble of thunder over the mountains to the west rolled over them and at the same moment Kwinn knew exactly what had happened.

Buckshot had defied Bandit. He had refused to settle

down in what he had considered an unsafe place. He had left his brothers and gone off to hunt without them.

Did Buckshot believe that, if he returned with some scraps of food, Bandit would be impressed and change his mind? Did Buckshot actually believe that Bandit would appreciate this rebellious behavior?

Buckshot turned from Kwinn. He lowered his head. He should have known better. Bandit was pack leader; he could tolerate hunger and he could tolerate pain but he could never – especially now in the dazed and weakened state in which he found himself, tolerate disrespect. The reins of this journey, the decisions of when and where to stop, to rest, to continue, were his; only in death would he surrender them.

Kwinn and Buckshot stood without moving, their minds linked as the vivid scene played out before them.

Bandit had awakened to find Buckshot gone and a light fog over the trail. Slowly he stood and looked around. It was getting dark. Francis, who had been sleeping beside him struggled up, shook off a few drops of rain, and stood blinking uncertainly, waiting for direction.

Bandit turned. So this was how his life would end – alone, with no one but Francis beside him. Well, never mind. As long as his heart held out, he could delay it – delay the shame of it, delay the crumbling of his bones to it, push back, push hard against it. Fight!

Molly took a step, nickered and nudged Kwinn's shoulder. But then she quieted as the moment stilled, a dark shadow silent as stone beside him. The three, human, horse and coyote, seemed frozen in time. It was raining; soon it would be completely dark. But no one stirred as they watched the vision of what must have been the final moments of a mighty soul.

Bandit had begun to walk. Pain had sharpened his mind. He would find his sister and bring her home. That was his mission; he would complete it.

It was then, right at the moment that Bandit had begun his final walk, that a truck already loaded with the corpses of 20 dead coyotes appeared out of nowhere, raced up beside him and screeched to a halt.

CHAPTER 13

The two hunters who shot Bandit and dragged his body to their truck, lowering the tailgate and attempting to heave him in among their other trophies, had no idea until that moment that Francis even existed.

He came out of nowhere, out of the shadowed ravine – the ghost of a memory, pencil-thin, a black streak out of their past bringing balance, bringing justice now, NOW – pure and naked into the night – BAM!

He sprang at one of the hunters, tearing his pants leg off at the knee, snarling and whipping around him with such speed that neither man could get a decent look at him. Francis may have been little, but Francis was fast – so fast he was impossible to stop. A tornado. A whirlwind. And then – gone. Just like that. Gone.

For a moment there was silence.

"Hey, get over here," the other hunter who was left holding the top half of Bandit was still struggling to hoist him up to the floor of the truck bed. He turned, his eyes searching the darkness. "How many of 'em are there?"

"I don't know, two or three. Maybe his whole pack!" The

first hunter was breathing heavily. He began to limp towards the front of the truck, "I'll get my gun. Hold on"

The second hunter looked around, "His pack can go to hell." He paused. There was sill no sign of Francis. "This big one must weigh 60 pounds," he called to his friend, raising his voice as if it made a difference, as if Francis would be put off by it. Again he searched the darkness. "Are you comin or what?"

"Where'd he go? The one who got me – where'd he go?" The first hunter was back with his rifle. He dropped it momentarily in order to help shove Bandit into the truck.

"How do I know?" The second hunter looked over his shoulder. "We got our twenty. Right? This here makes twenty-one." He grunted, "Shove him in further. We need to hide these varmints till we get home."

Both men were panting and sweating heavily as they reached together to lift and close the tailgate.

"Hold on; wait a minute," the first hunter reached into the truck, pushing the tailgate back down with his elbow. "I'll tell you what we need to hide." He grabbed Bandit by his bandaged leg and pulled him closer to the edge of the truck bed. "Get me something to tear this leg off. Looks like we shot somebody's dog!"

"What are you – crazy?" the second hunter began walking up to the cab. "Come on," he opened the door, "we'll tear his leg off later."

"I said, wait!" The first hunter leaned into the back of the truck and began rummaging around. "There's a hacksaw in here somewhere." Suddenly he laughed, pulling a rusty hatchet from the bottom of a long toolbox, "Maybe I'll just chop it off with this."

And then, it happened. Francis was back! So fast he was almost invisible, he tore out of the shadows in full-fledged attack-mode, leaping onto the hunter's back, ripping open his flannel shirt and tearing the skin on his back in a neat strip of raw flesh. In a moment, the hunter was on the ground, grasping for his gun, scrambling to his knees and firing blindly into the shadowed ravine from which he assumed Francis had come.

The other hunter jumped into the truck, pulled on the lights, and spun around next to his friend. "Get in," he called reaching across the cab and pushing open the passenger door, "Get in!" which the man on the ground was grateful to do, turning back first to slam shut the tailgate.

"Okay, all in," he said with relief, picturing the pile of carcasses in the truck bed. "At least we still got our twenty-one, bandaged leg and all!"

But it didn't matter how many bodies they had. The balance was soon to shift in the bloody bed of that hunters' truck. Because Francis, alive and well, was in there too.

CHAPTER 14

The hunters drove 60 miles before they stopped, planning to take a leak, get some gas and check in by phone with the backwoods country store that acted as headquarters for the bi-monthly coyote killing contests.

These contests, popular in several California counties before they were discontinued, served not only as entertainment but were said to have the practical value of limiting predator attacks on the state's many small farms and ranches – although, to be honest, this was secondary to the fun of the competition. The entry fee was $20 for a two man team and the prizes, both for count and weight, were a good chunk of the total collected.

Trouble was that, since word got out of their impending demise, these contests had been growing like crazy, each one bringing in dozens of unseasoned hunters with no real appreciation of the sport, many of whom were determined to cheat. They came early, setting up their fancy equipment days ahead of time, littering the land with outlawed snares, foot and leg-hold traps, even those disgusting body crushing contraptions that could squeeze the life right out an animal.

All of this sneaking around was pointless however. Contest rules were strict. The dead animals were carefully checked for any signs that traps or snares had been used, and the inner heat of each body was tested to be sure it had been killed within the permitted 48 hour time frame. No exceptions.

As for the locals, experience had taught them that even before the contest officially began, the coyotes would be long gone, having disappeared from all this nonsense without a trace, leaving the land suddenly empty and forcing the locals to travel many miles to get their kills in the time allowed.

The hunters, with Bandit and Francis behind them in the truck bed, pulled into a large off-road travel center slightly before nine p.m. They parked in the darkest area they could find at the back of the lot under two burned out pole-lights.

"Maybe we should put a tarp over 'em." The driver glanced towards the back of the truck. The men were still inside the cab, trying to get presentable. Francis' victim was working with a pocket knife to match his long pants leg to the shorter one.

"For God's sake, Chuck, they're dead. Gimme a vest," he said, more interested in covering his own back than the backs of a heap of dead coyotes. "Son of a gun ripped my shirt, tore me up good."

"Here," The driver tossed his friend a cowhide vest from the back section of the cab. "What happened to the kill blocks? We need to go back there and stick 'em in the varmints' mouths fore their jaws lock up." He reached to open his door.

"Forget it." The injured hunter turned to look over his

shoulder toward the back of the truck. "No one can see what we got back there anyway." He got out of the truck and chuckled softly to himself. "It's not like them bodies plan to advertise their selves."

No. Not yet. But there had been a whole lot going on in the back of that truck for the last hour. The only reason it was quiet now was because two pairs of ears had gone up as the truck stopped, listening intently to the voices in the cab, their copper bodies low, side by side on the floor of the truck just inside the tailgate, undistinguishable from the carcasses behind them, and not wanting to disturb the one who lay barely alive between them.

This one, the one that was barely alive, was listening too – but you'd never know it.

As happens in most killing rooms, gas chambers, war zones, forest fires, earthquakes and floods, not everyone dies. This gives hope to all those worried about a nuclear holocaust, a world wide pandemic, invaders from space, etc. Not everyone will die. Once the dust has settled and the sky has cleared above the new reality, there will always be at least one pair of ears that go up, straight up. Maybe two.

It had been quite a night for Francis and it wasn't over yet. Examining Bandit by sniffing and licking him all over as soon as the truck was safely moving, Francis decided to confront the bleeding from his brother's chest first by cleaning it, and then by gently biting the torn flesh where the hunter's bullet had entered – trying futilely to coax it out.

When this failed and the wound, with Bandit's heart still faintly throbbing beneath it, began to slowly refill with blood, he decided as a last resort to lay on top of it – crawling right over Bandit's stomach to let his weight press down upon the wound, holding Bandit's lifeblood in with all the pressure he could muster.

So concentrated were Francis' efforts to save his brother's life, he never noticed the first tentative movements of the one coyote in the pile of carcasses behind him who was still alive. When he finally did notice, he refused to let it concern him. If someone back there had been clever enough to fake his own death, good for him. But it was probably nothing; dead bodies often moved.

After a few more minutes, Francis lifted his head and looked back over his shoulder. The lone survivor had disentangled himself from the heap of bodies around him and was standing shyly a few feet away, staring at Francis with huge shell-shocked eyes as the truck rumbled along and he swayed back and forth with it. Francis watched him. He hoped it would be obvious to the newcomer that he was very busy. They could meet another time – not now.

The newcomer took a shaky step. Physically he seemed intact. He was just too horrified by what he had been through to know what to do next.

Francis' heart melted. The newcomer moved carefully around to Bandit's other side and lay down next to him. After a few minutes, he pushed his back up against Bandit's back, stretched out on his side, and sighed. He would help. He would keep Bandit warm. He would be friend.

When two minds are moving in sync about what must be done, no words are needed to form a plan. They had almost an hour – Francis and Friend, with Bandit between them. Their minds were now perfectly in sync. They were keenly awake, alert, conscious of every sound, every movement in the cab of the truck.

So when the engine slowed to a stop, idled, and then silenced completely, their ears went up. They waited. And when, fifteen minutes later, the driver and his friend could be heard approaching, their footsteps crunching in the loose gravel as they made their way to the back of the truck, Francis and Friend were ready.

As the tailgate came down, they leapt into the dark like shadows, fast, over the heads of the two hunters who crouched involuntarily, arms up to shield themselves from whatever flew above, as one would crouch to avoid bats. But these weren't bats – swinging mid-air to return, smashing into the hunters, knocking them to the ground, double shadows, moving and blurring in the darkness, snarling and ripping, enacting the revenge of the wild upon their human predators.

It was a nightmare scenario for the men; one of them tripped and fell, the other fired blindly and then tried to run but in his confusion hit the side of the truck, dropped his weapon and slid to the ground.

And then it got worse. One of the animals (they had no idea how many were attacking them,) approached the newly fallen hunter, grasped his rifle and clenched it between his jaws. The sounds from his throat were the sounds of Satan himself, or so the two men believed.

In the total darkness it was impossible to see. Both men began backing up, still on their knees as the snarling creature came closer and closer, looming over them as they recoiled in horror and as Francis, who had been hurt but who hardly felt it, silently leapt back into the truck, pulling Bandit across the open tailgate and onto the black ground with a thud.

The hunters never noticed. They had no idea what the wild animals that attacked them wanted, or that any of their kills had been removed from the truck. They knew only that they wanted out of there, clawing the dirt to retrieve their rifles, scrambling and running to the front of the truck, climbing in and cussing loudly because even now, safe in the truck, there was no way to retaliate because their attackers had vanished.

The hunters took off with a screech, the truck's tailgate still down, unable to speak of the horror of their experience, each one silently vowing to stay up north from now on, where things were more sane.

After all, they were lucky to be alive. They could dump the dog with the bandaged leg later; he just wasn't worth it anymore. Even without him, they still had their twenty – didn't they?

HA HA HA. I don't think so.

CHAPTER 15

It was close to midnight when Rufus, traveling south along the #395, a desolate stretch of desert highway, saw the truck. He stopped and listened. Not a sound.

Rufus walked onto the empty highway, paused, and then padded quietly up to the rank smelling vehicle that sat in darkness on the shoulder of northbound #395, its occupants asleep.

The smell of death in the bed of the truck was strong. Rufus stopped, his stomach convulsing from the stench. But still he continued closer. Had he scented Bandit? He wasn't sure.

Rufus backed up until he was about ten yards from the truck. He crouched low. A dense fog was settling over the desert. Rufus gathered his strength, his soul, all of the force that nature had given him for moments like …THIS! And Rufus' body lengthened into a long low streak of power, and he ran, and he leapt … up … UP!

Rufus' landing in the bed of the truck was light. No one stirred as he investigated the bodies, searching for his brothers, searching for any sign of life at all. But there was none.

Rufus left the bed of the truck as quietly and as gracefully as he had entered it. He stood a short distance away, began to turn to leave but then stopped and turned back. Perhaps Bandit was no longer there. But the mangled bodies in the bed of that truck were also kin.

Rufus stood like a ghost in the middle of the road as a lone black vehicle approached, its fog lights barely visible – pale halos of yellow that looked to Rufus like the eyes of a spirit.

Rufus didn't move.

"What's that, on the road? Slow up."

"Must be an animal of some sort. Looks like something's wrong with him." The vehicle stopped. "Damn if it's a dog! What's he doin way out here?"

"Look. There's a truck over there, on the shoulder. See it? Let's check it out."

"Yeah but I don't like it. Something's not right. I'll back up and swing over behind it – run the plates."

Rufus watched as one of the officers exited the vehicle and approached the back of the truck on the passenger side. He flicked on his flashlight and stopped to look over the side of the truck bed, "Geeze," he said quietly, shaking his head as if he could shake the vision of all those bodies from his mind.

The other officer was out of the car now, approaching with his weapon drawn. The blue lights from his radio cast an eerie veil over the inside of the patrol car. "What is it?" He paused. "What's that stink?" But he didn't need an answer. He knew exactly what it was.

The first officer straightened, "Let's wake them up. See if they have a license for this. Did their plates check out?"

"Yeah. But ... there's a call out for a dark blue pickup seen down at the Travel Stop this side of the #58. Discharging a firearm – close proximity to a fuel station. Also dumped some carcasses back of the parking lot. That's two violations right there."

There was some stirring inside the cab. The first officer approached, his weapon by his side. Rufus, forgotten by the officers, was invisible – watching.

"Ok – out of the vehicle, hands up where I can see 'em. What you got in there? Been drinkin?"

Soon both hunters were out of the truck, being herded by the officers back to their patrol car where at least there was some faint light.

Rufus sent his thoughts once more to the silent truck, his dead cousins. He looked up through the fog into the black sky. All right. It was done. It was not enough, but it was something. Maybe, in the long ... long story of everyone's life and everyone's death, it mattered.

The postscript to this event is a strange one. In spite of the write-ups the hunters received, in spite of the tickets, the fines and mandatory court appearance they would face for their actions, they were smiling broadly when the police let them go, an hour later. Why? Because, hey, they still had their twenty, didn't they?

Really? um ... stop laughing, Friend.

CHAPTER 16

By the time Buckshot, traveling alone, reached the Travel Center it was almost dawn and although he was elated to discover his brothers, the scene he encountered was a shock: Francis bloody and wounded lying next to Bandit whose eyes were closed as if in death while one bony, growling coyote stood over them, eyes glinting and lips curled at Buckshot.

The three had been discovered the previous night by an assistant cook who had been taking out the trash and was scanning the dark lot for whoever had used a firearm back there, not far from a wagon full of propane tanks, the implications of which had raised concern among the rest of the staff.

The young cook had been shocked to find the three bodies huddled together on edge of the lot – dogs or coyotes he couldn't tell, one possibly dead – an unmoving lump of dark fur, a second one smaller, lying on his side with several raw wounds, but conscious – ears up, watching.

The cook paused. The third animal, obviously coyote, was trying to stand, growling, his yellow eyes narrowed to slits. Soon he was poised like a ragged skeleton over the other two as if to protect them – although it was possible, the cook decided, that this one was in a state of confusion so huge he had no clear idea of what he was doing.

It would have been funny if it weren't so sad. The animals were barley half grown, seven months at the most.

The young man crouched down before the protector and offered him some fresh beef from the plastic trash bag he was still holding. When there was no response he offered the meat to Francis, who sniffed at it and seemed at least slightly interested. Eventually, the two conscious animals were coaxed off the lot to a safer spot, a protected hollow partially hidden within a stand of desert saltbush, each canine testing the ground suspiciously before settling in and allowing Bandit to be gently pushed between them as they growled and huffed solicitously.

When Buckshot first approached, all three had been asleep. A blanket had been laid over them and the faint, first light from an overcast sky had barely penetrated the protected recess where their benefactor had left them.

One at a time, Francis and then Friend, awakened to acknowledge Buckshot's presence. Francis huffed a friendly greeting. Friend, suspicious as usual, struggled to resume his threatening stance over Bandit, but then, taking a cue from Francis, stopped growling and uncurled his lip. Finally he left Bandit and sat down. When nothing happened he shifted his weight, looked back at Francis and gave Buckshot a tentative tail wag.

But Buckshot was frozen, his eyes glassed over.

Francis understood. Buckshot was terrified that Bandit was dead; it was too much to bear; he could not accept it.

Because although he was greatly relieved to see Francis, and although he seemed ready to accept the newcomer's shy greeting, for his own sanity he could not approach what seemed to be the dead and broken body of the brother who had been his eyes.

Francis was familiar with Buckshot's particular form of denial and waited patiently while his brother turned and began to pace, came back and rubbed his eye, then walked away again, stopping at a safe distance before turning to begin the routine again.

After a few rounds of this, Francis dragged himself closer to Bandit and laid his head over Bandit's neck, breathing heavily into his ear.

Buckshot couldn't help but look. He came closer and stood transfixed with his legs slightly apart, his head lowered, and the black pupils of his eyes opened so wide no other color could be seen.

Bandit twitched. He opened one eye.

Buckshot went ballistic with joy. He kissed Francis all over; he kissed Bandit all over; he even kissed the newcomer – not all over of course, but lavishly enough, a little on the face, a little on the ears…. So contagious was Buckshot's joy that Friend began a little dance of his own, head down, pawing the earth and bowing to show his submission to Buckshot.

But Buckshot didn't like that part of it – the submission part. He was not the leader; he was neither wise enough nor strong enough. Only Bandit was leader. He, Buckshot, could be Bandit's partner, his lieutenant, his second-in-command. But he could never *be* Bandit; he could never take Bandit's place. And, anyway, his eye hurt him.

Some might say what Buckshot did next was foolish. But Buckshot was still trying to cope; he wasn't completely himself yet. If Tobias were still alive, or if his mother were still alive, he could have called to them for help. But they were gone – too far away to hear.

So he trotted a few dozen yards away from his brothers, crossed an empty lot and climbed a small mound of dirt on the edge of the open desert. Then, in spite of the proximity of the travel plaza and the scattering of homes and ranches around it, in spite of the repercussions his call could have in such a semi-populated area, he called.

He sang his prayer knowing that there was no one in this world to tell him what to do, to tell him how to save Bandit and how to help Francis, no one under the vast grey silent sky above him who would answer him call.

But maybe someone above the sky would hear – someone farther than eyes could see. Maybe *that* someone would hear! So, on the slim chance that he would be heard, on the slim chance that someone in the distant heavens would care about his sad predicament, Buckshot lifted up his throat and sang. He sang his whole story, his whole need. And then he sang his thanks.

It made no sense. Or, depending upon who you are, it made all the sense in the world.

CHAPTER 17

Rufus, traveling southbound and still following the #395, approached the lone travel center just as the sun made a brief appearance before sinking again behind the thickly clouded sky. He was less than a mile west of the plaza, heading south. In the distance he could see the #58; it was empty; his path was clear.

And then he heard Buckshot's call. Rufus stopped, his heart pounding. The travel center, barely visible in early light, lay as still and silent as a photograph. Rufus began to move closer to Buckshot's call but he could not see him; nor could he see his other brothers.

Once more he stopped. To his south lay thirty miles of open land, an easy journey before the land darkened into the treacherous trails and forested hills that held a trapped and terrified Jewel. She trusted him. She was waiting for him.

Buckshot needed help but Jewel also needed help.

So, being true to the wisdom of the tall and mysterious magi with whom he had slept in Father Bernardo's stable, Rufus decided to pause his journey right there, to lie down and to be still.

Rufus, remember, was a thinker, but at times like this thinking wasn't enough. Thinking, in fact, could get in the way. Instead, Rufus decided simply to trust. He would wait patiently and like the magi before him he would open his mind so that the answer to where he should go would come to him.

Rufus closed his eyes. He was on a low hill overlooking the Travel Center and the empty desert beyond it. All was touched with a stillness that seemed to hold the earth in perfect balance as night released her claim and morning light emerged to touch the land.

But the fullness of day was not to come – not yet. A long low cloud appeared and spread until it filled the sky. And then as Rufus sank into sleep the cloud became a slow descending fog that dropped a curtain over everything.

Rufus slept in perfect trust. The dream he was to dream would fall with ease into his mind – but not into his mind alone. This vision would spread its wings, seeking out the mind of another and hover ghostlike above it, waiting until that mind also would open and relax.

Kwinn was camped 20 miles east of the Travel Center. Most of the night he had been praying for Buckshot's safety, wondering why he had disappeared so quickly from the bloody scene where Bandit had been taken, vanishing like a spirit in the pouring rain. But Buckshot had been intent upon tracking the truck that had taken his brother, caring only for that, only for Bandit, which was right and good.

So Kwinn and Molly had been left alone.

They had done their best with only Kwinn's flashlight, following the muddy ruts the truck had made for almost a mile before it swung suddenly south, heading straight to the black and shining pavement of the #58.

As far as Kwinn could tell, the killers had turned west onto the highway but from that point on there were no tracks to follow; all that he and Molly could do was to continue parallel to the highway, stopping at each turn-off to search in the rain for some sign of Buckshot's prints or at least a trace of tread-mark from the hunters' truck.

Finally, the rain had stopped. Kwinn and Molly slowed their pace, listening. The highway lay still beside them; there was not a single vehicle on it. The sky and earth were covered with a blackness so intense there was no way to tell where one ended and the other began.

But there is safety in this kind of darkness – a permission to breathe deeply, permission to relax the muscles in your chest. There is an understanding that whatever else is out there, friend or enemy, it also has been embraced, enclosed, made safe by darkness. So just as the other creatures around them, invisible in the totality of blackness, gave in to the night and surrendered to it, so Molly and Kwinn surrendered also.

Kwinn and Molly were dozing peacefully when the first hint of dawn lightened the sky. Kwinn, barely awake, lifted his eyes to see a long low cloud approaching from the west. As he watched it filled the sky and began to lower over him. Throughout the night he had prayed for guidance. Now, it had come. His eyes closed.

Kwinn's dream was this:

He was alone walking under a black sky in a strange empty land. Beside him was the highway but there were no cars on it, no lights, no sign of life. Suddenly a dense fog settled over him and he could see nothing. Kwinn stopped. For a moment he could hear only his own heartbeat. Then, through the fog he could see a figure approaching. Kwinn stared in amazement. Tobias?

The mysterious image began to lead Kwinn back the way that he had come, urging him to turn and retrace his steps to a narrow path of broken pavement that branched from the highway and headed almost invisibly at an angle going north/northwest and disappearing into the night.

When Kwinn balked at going backwards, the image of Tobias came closer and pressed against him, leaning him irresistibly into the desired turn, his once familiar eyes magnetic with expression and confidence. *This is the way*, he seemed to be saying. *Follow me.*

And then Kwinn remembered Tobias. He had found him keeping guard outside an occupied coyote den, freshly dug with newborn pups and their mother inside. Tobias was whimpering, confused. *She won't come out,* he seemed to be saying. *She comes just so far, looks at me, and then goes right back in.*

Kwinn had smiled. This was a dog, not a coyote; he must not know that as the pups' father he was expected to bring food to the den every day for at least the first week of the pups' life. Their mother would never leave her pups alone to hunt for food herself.

So Kwinn had gone for a bird, felled it, and brought it to the den himself. He moved Tobias aside and placed it at the den entrance. Then he guarded it from Tobias until the pups' mother appeared and pulled it inside. Once he saw her,

Kwinn understood easily why Tobias loved her. He saw her gentleness with Tobias, her patience.

She knew that Tobias would learn quickly; he would be a good father to their pups. And she was right. Kwinn had checked back several times and Tobias was always on duty, guarding her fresh meal at the mouth of the den until she appeared to retrieve it.

And then, suddenly Kwinn remembered Mira, and he remembered the grave of Tobias. So how could this be Tobias leading him?

Kwinn turned and there was Molly beside him. For some reason, in this dream, it never occurred to Kwinn to mount and ride Molly. Instead, they both walked behind Tobias under a vast silent sky, the broken pavement underfoot. Finally, Kwinn stopped to rest. He sat down to pray but he was very weak. His head bowed.

When Kwinn awoke he realized that he and Molly were a much greater distance from the highway than he remembered. He stood and looked around. And then he saw it: a small piece of broken pavement, almost completely buried in the sand, heading west into what appeared to be nothing. Then, another. And another.

So Kwinn and Molly began a series of hesitant steps – a path in the middle of nowhere, a shortcut that would lead them to Bandit and Francis just as the morning light broke through the disappearing haze above them.

Buckshot, back on the hill from which he had called so earnestly to Heaven, saw the approaching figures in the distance. He shook his head and squinted cautiously, and then, in case he was mistaken, emerged at a conservative trot to greet them.

When Kwinn and Molly, escorted by Buckshot, arrived at the space where Francis and Bandit were hidden, three men who had come on foot from the Travel Center were standing a few feet from the open end of the circle of protecting brush, talking in low tones about its new residents.

"Good day, Gentlemen," Kwinn reined in Molly as she looked with longing at the stand of saltbush, their tender leaves (aka cattle spinach) an enchanting sight. "I see you've discovered my dogs,"

Kwinn had yet to see into the protected grove but since Buckshot had led him there, he assumed that his brothers were hidden within.

"They're bad hurt, both of 'em," the youngest of the three men spoke, moving to Molly and distractedly pulling a stem of leaves from the nearest bush for her. He looked up at Kwinn, "I brung 'em some food and water last night but one can't eat – he's pretty far gone."

Kwinn dismounted, not bothering to ground-tie Molly, leaving her free to chomp. He began walking towards the opening in the bush. An older man joined him. "I was think-ing to put at least one of 'em out of his misery," the older man said as they entered the small grove and saw Bandit mo-tionless, with Francis stretched out half across him. "Sheriff hears of this, he'll end it quick for 'em both." He paused, looking at Kwinn, "What do you think?"

"No, I'll take it from here." Kwinn glanced at the hand-gun holstered on the man's hip, "I'll send for some help, and a truck." Kwinn moved closer to Bandit and Francis; he crouched down to study them. "Meantime," he said, looking back over his shoulder, "I'll stay here with them."

As the two older men began their walk back to the Travel Center, the youngest approached Kwinn. He crouched down next to him. "There's another one," he said quietly. "There were three – right?"

The young man's eyes scanned the brush and while Kwinn watched, he half-stood searching the desert scrub, the desolate land on either side of the protected grove. Kwinn met his eyes. The young man whispered, "He's kinda coyote lookin – pure-like. Know what I mean?"

Kwinn nodded, saying nothing. After a few moments he stood, taking out his phone. "Service out here?" he said, turning away from Bandit and Francis and walking to the grove opening where Buckshot stood guard.

"Yep, mostly there is," the boy followed Kwinn. "See the lot over there? Right under that pole light – see it? That's a good spot, right there."

Kwinn smiled. "Thanks for your help." He sighed, "These animals are young, orphans, just tryin to live, just want a chance."

"Yeah, I figured," the boy smiled back. "Like us, I guess." And then he quietly turned and walked away.

Good person, Kwinn thought, watching the small thin figure crossing the empty parking lot alone. *Just past half-grown, but wiser than most who are twice his age.*

Like you, Buckshot, he said without speaking, and then he smiled. Buckshot looked down, turning so Kwinn could not see him. And then he smiled also.

Rufus' ears went up. He lifted his head and yawned peacefully. He stood and stretched. That human friend of

Buckshot's wasn't easy to convince. He looked across the desert and saw Kwinn and Molly standing with Buckshot by a clump of brush just behind the Travel Center. For a moment he watched them. Well, maybe it wasn't much but he had done what he could. He turned and began to lope south. Time to find Jewel.

CHAPTER 18

The same white whisper of fog that played across Rufus' eyes as he crossed the #58, was drifting in long tattered veils across the final miles of his journey, clouding the hills that began to rise before him and making the mountains of the San Bernardino range invisible. He had less than 40 miles to go.

The forest where Jewel lay was within this cloud. She had stopped struggling to free herself from the twisted cable of the snare that gripped her right below her neck, wrapping under her shoulder and digging into her chest, knowing this would only cause more pain.

She was desperately thirsty. At first she had been able to reach a nearby rock for moisture and to lick the moss that grew along its base. But then there was nothing. Her neck was strained, her head ached, and the pain in her shoulder was constant.

Most cruel of all, on the morning of the second day she had heard voices, young voices, the laughing voices of hikers, and she had hoped they might discover and help her. She had tried to bark, whimpering and whining until finally two of the youngsters had peered through the trees and threaded their way to where she lay.

But they were afraid, talking in whispers, backing up when she lifted her head. "She could have rabies," one of them said, pointing to the dry foam on the edges of Jewel's mouth. "Maybe she's violent; don't get too close."

"She doesn't look violent," the other replied. "She's probably just thirsty." He paused. "Coyotes are shy of people." He turned to look at his friend. "Aren't they?"

"All I know is that they're unpredictable. She could be faking so she could attack us."

The taller of the boys approached Jewel. He bent to study her but straightened when he noticed her eyes, bulging and bloodshot as they rolled toward him. "Yeah, you're right." he said. "She looks scary."

So that was it. They left quickly, worried that the trapper might appear. The snare, in spite of the way it had entangled its victim, was someone else's property.

"Sorry," the tall one said as they turned to go. He gave Jewel a brief, regretful look and tossed a small bag of trail-mix across the ground to where she lay.

Jewel spent the rest of the day trying to reach that little bag, straining for it, scrambling with her thin back legs and pulling sporadically with the one front leg that was still functional; the other front leg entangled by the snare lay numbed and swollen beneath her.

The trap had come as a shock. Its loop was nine inches in diameter, probably intended to snare a larger animal and yet it had been set low over the forest path, disguised by grass. Jewel, unable to see it, had been following a rabbit's scent, running close to the ground, her eyes partially closed, her leading leg extended parallel to her head so that both went into the loop together. And zoom! She was lifted, swung around, flung against a tree and left limp at its base on a brambly heap of thick vines and dead branches.

After two days in the snare, Jewel knew what any further movement could do to her aching throat and the strained and rasping windpipe within it. But she was so thirsty, so desperately thirsty for whatever moisture the little bag on the ground might hold, that on the evening of that second day, she foolishly made one last attempt.

As Jewel sunk into unconsciousness, she dreamed of rain – blessed rain, lifesaving rain.

It had been two weeks since her mother had died and Jewel had never felt so alone. When a bolt of lightening had split the huge Oak tree behind the cabin where Mira had left her, her only instinct had been to escape. She had flown through the window, hit the ground, and run for her life. Outside, she knew, was to be cherished while inside could become a trap.

So Jewel ran, straight and long, not thinking, not reasoning, just running. She ran until it was dark. She ran until the storm no longer threatened, and the neighborhood had changed. She ran until she was completely lost.

Jewel was small, the size of Francis, so she slipped easily into yards, melted behind trash cans, faded among tree trunks. But most of the time she was too terrified to get that close to humans, their yards or homes.

If someone saw her or called to her, she would just turn and stare at them. She would feel dizzy trying to recall what she should do, where she should go. She desperately wanted to do the right thing but instead she would stand stupidly on the road before them, too paralyzed with fear to even run away.

Jewel was yelled at, clapped at, honked at, and almost run down a number of times before she got the hang of things and before the cars and dwellings diminished and the road began to lift beyond them.

Once she had suddenly come upon a young girl walking alone on the same shadowed road that she was on. The girl seemed fearful, her hand on a slender can she held by her side. Jewel stopped, her heart thumping. The girl was the same size and shape as Mira. She moved like Mira. Jewel took a tentative step toward the girl. Her ears went up; she wagged her tail just a little as she moved closer. Could it be Mira?

The spray of chemicals from the girl's extended hand did more than surprise Jewel, sting her eyes and turn her away. It shocked her. She knew that most humans were to be avoided, especially loud humans. But the cruelty of quiet humans, humans that looked like Mira, was devastating. Why would one of them hurt her? What had she done?

Jewel soon began heading for the mountain foothills. She had caught glimpses of them as she ran, appearing briefly between houses and trees as they rolled and climbed, blending into forests rich with the enticing smells of Spring.

So when the road wound up and up into the mountains, Jewel gladly followed. For several days she rested. Rabbits and gophers were plentiful and the sound of water seeping through exquisitely thin sheets of melting ice to skim and slide over moss covered rocks was never far away. She slept under great oak trees, safely curled between their roots. She awakened to the songs of hundreds of birds and stood amazed as she watched them moving among the long and budding branches above her.

Jewel happened upon the new house by accident – trotting down the narrow road, shocked to see Jacob's truck in the yard. But she was shy of him by then, too shy to approach him. The days she had spent alone made him seem strangely alien so she kept her distance, watched him in secret, peering out at him from behind the trees as he packed up his tools and got into his truck and left.

For the rest of that day she hung around, scenting all over the property, drinking from the familiar creek and finally curling up in the alcove by a side door to sleep. When morning came she waited hopefully but when no one appeared she walked down the road like a shadow, slid into the woods, and disappeared.

It took her three more days to find the lake. It was nestled in a forested refuge with plenty of wildlife and few humans on the trails. There had been other lakes along the way but there were always roads and vehicles nearby.

Once she was forced deep into the woods by a monster truck that must have seen her from the road below. It had swerved suddenly, grinding gears and rocking up the muddy hill to where she watched in horror as it plowed through roots and brush to follow her, stopping only when the trees formed a wall that it could not penetrate.

But Jewel did not give up her search for peace. She continued through the woods until she found her solitary lake surrounded by pine and juniper, its water crystal clear and deliciously cold. Best of all, schools of silver fish skimmed about in the shallow places under ledges and along the tree lined banks.

Jewel had never seen, never encountered a hunter's trap. At first she panicked, threw herself around desperately as the cable tightened and cut into her flesh. But soon she learned to be still. The cable that held her was thick and twisted. Even if she could get a grip on it, she could not bite through it. So all she could do was wait, calling over and over to Rufus, but less and less hopeful that he would appear.

But at least she could dream. Perhaps a dream can be a form of hope – a kind of prayer that one has no idea she is praying but that can be very real indeed.

Just after dawn the same day that Kwinn discovered Bandit and Francis, the brief but powerful spring storm that had soaked the desert the night before was opening its second phase over the mountains to the south. By sunrise, with Rufus still many miles away, it had found our sleeping Jewel and blessed her dreams of water with the real thing.

CHAPTER 19

A mixed blessing, that spring storm – a regular San Bernardino downpour. Trappers in most areas of California are required to check their traps daily. Even in the state's most remote areas a trap cannot remain unchecked for more than 72 hours, and in a further attempt to minimize suffering, a trap's victim once discovered must be killed or freed as soon as possible.

Enforcement of these rules, however, has always been difficult especially in rugged terrain with few officers to patrol. Thankfully, most experienced trappers follow the rules, setting their traps and snares safely away from footpaths and hiking trails, and honoring their duty to check on them daily.

Obviously, the trapper who caught Jewel was an amateur, or worse. His trap, with no I.D. attached to it, was set dangerously close to a hiking trail. Well hidden and obviously homemade, it was a hazard to numerous non-target animals as well as to the adventurous human.

But even if the trapper whose ignorance had entangled Jewel was starting off that third morning to inspect his trap, the rushing mud and water from the storm would have changed his mind.

It rained all day. By noon, Rufus had left the open desert behind, and in another hour he was cautiously approaching the highway underpass that led to the lake where his sister lay. Traffic was light; the sky was grey and the windshield wipers of passing cars moved to their own rhythm. Rufus trotted into the tunnel and out again unnoticed.

Soon some greenery appeared, some trees and thickets, a place to drink, a place to rest. But no – there was no stopping Rufus now. All that remained was to search for food, to scent along the roads and grasses as he ran, to look for scraps – discarded meat, anything of substance that he could bring to Jewel.

By 2 p.m., the worst of the storm was over and the rain had morphed into a fine shower. Rufus slowed his pace. He lifted his head and listened.

How did he know that his sister was near? That's the mystery, isn't it? But he did know. He just knew.

Mira and Ben, however, felt no such assurance that this was the day they would find little Jewel. They had left home at dawn, hoping that the darkening sky and slow threatening rumbles of thunder would come to nothing. Even as the rain began, they ignored it.

But when mid-morning found them dealing with the same constant downpour that was blessing Jewel, their confidence in finding her began to slip, and by noon they were soaked, and almost ready to give up.

Almost.

Finally, they had to stop. It seemed foolish to continue.

The trails around the hidden lakes that they had set out hoping to explore would soon be full of mud and probably impassible. Well, they could explore one more, just one.

It was early afternoon as Mira and Ben approached that final lake. They had no idea – how could they know? – how close they were to the very spot where Jewel lay.

But then, everything changed. The rumbling above them stopped and the sky seemed to lighten. They looked up, amazed. The rain had become a harmless shower.

Mira and Ben proceeded slowly. Even the horses seemed hesitant. Was this the calm before another storm? They didn't know. They knew only that they needed to rest, to consider carefully what they should do.

So when their horses decided to suddenly leave the trail, turning into the trees and heading for a steep hill that overlooked the lake, Mira and Ben allowed their equine guardians to have their way.

It was a good choice. From their lookout Mira and Ben could wait out the changing weather in comfort. And, by the way, arguing with horses is never a good idea.

So there they sat, resigned, nodding under the dripping branches of a stately ponderosa pine from which their horses, content at last, refused to budge. It was almost mid afternoon. They rested.

Aside from the steady humming of the light but continuing rain, the forest was immensely still. All tours had been canceled; roads that had temporarily opened at dawn had been reclosed, their yellow barricades set in place by two of the park's four officers while the other two proceeded on foot to monitor the trails for hikers quick to panic when their way was blocked by fast moving water or broken tree limbs, making familiar ways impassable.

It was late in the day when the rain stopped for good. One of the park officers, making a final check for whatever damage the storm may have caused, found Jewel. When the downpour began in earnest, she had struggled to get to higher ground, her head stretched awkwardly into some thick bramble above her. A man with less keen vision might have missed her completely.

"Good God, look at you!" The officer crouched towards Jewel, separating the branches that partially covered her. "Maybe I can ...," he bent down further trying to wedge his fingers under the cable while he ran his hand around her shoulder and under her leg as far as he dared, looking for a built-in stop that he might be able to loosen. Jewel didn't move, watching him through huge and frightened eyes.

"Can't do it," he was breathing heavily. "Hang on, Girl," he glanced down, wincing, as he slowly pulled his fingers from beneath the cutting twist of wire. He stood, talking to himself as he studied the snare, "I'll think of something ..."

The officer took a breath. He turned slightly and reached for his radio but froze suddenly when what appeared to be a wild dog came plunging out of the undergrowth, lips curled in a threatening snarl.

"Whoa! Easy, Boy," the officer instinctively straightened his arms, opening his hands to show they were empty. Rufus moved closer, a slow growl rising in his throat.

The officer moved back a few feet.

Rufus, his eyes still locked on the officer, sidestepped closer to Jewel. It was then that the officer noticed the remains of a carcass hidden in the brambles above Jewel's head.

The officer smiled, "Well, looks like we both want to help her, Big Fella," he said softly, sliding back another foot into the tangled brush. "Don't worry, I won't touch her again."

He looked down, avoiding Rufus' penetrating gaze – an intermittent threat still rumbling in the dog's throat. His voice was low, almost conversational, "Now … here's the story. You need to let me …" he carefully took out his radio, "make a call." He breathed heavily. "That's all I'm doing – see?" he looked up, "so we can help her." Rufus didn't move; he was watching the officer intently, listening to every word.

"Rodney, hey – this is Miles. I've got an injured coyote here; yeah, illegal snare – no I.D. – got her by the neck and twisted under her shoulder. I need a cable cutter, not wire – no, I said cable. Yeah, well, we'll worry about that later. I'd check it out some more but she's being guarded – now get this; there's a dog guarding her – big, red coat, looks like a retriever type, the kind duck hunters use. He's serious; I can't get near her. Bring whatever you've got to scare him off. Yeah, I know. You'll have to hike in. I'm by the lake, west of the footpath on the south side where the creek branches into the woods, right there at the branch.

"Listen, I don't want to kill this dog. I don't know what his problem is but he's feral for sure, no collar – nothing. He's got me trapped here, threatening to jump me if I move too fast. If I can distract him and get my gun out, I'll fire over his head, try to spook him. If he comes at me though, I'll have to kill him."

"Well, it's just you and me, Boy." Miles casually lowered himself to the ground. He laid his radio beside him and turned slowly so that he was at an angle to Rufus and no longer facing him.

Carefully, inch-by-inch, he removed his revolver from the holster under his vest. Then, with the gun on his lap, he turned to face Rufus.

But Rufus wasn't interested. The dog, his back to Miles, was leaning over Jewel, licking her and making sounds of encouragement as he anxiously swayed back and forth, his long tail wagging just slightly, as if hoping his greeting would be contagious. He seemed to have forgotten Miles completely.

Miles relaxed. He watched amazed as Jewel opened her eyes. *They're young – both of them*, he was thinking. *She's coyote, just a pup, and yet ... and yet ... somehow she trusts this dog that's almost twice her size.* Miles studied the two canines. *Must be related*, he decided. *Brother and sister? Is that even possible?*

The rain had stopped but the peace of the moment was soon to be broken. Two officers, who believed they were coming to Mile's rescue, crept silently closer along the footpath, their movements masked by thick new growth that formed a fence-like barrier along the trail. So when they crashed through the brush, yelling loudly with their guns drawn, it was a shock. Rufus spun around, preparing to attack. One of the new officers saw him, "There he is! You okay, Miles?"

But before Miles could answer, that same officer took aim to fire – not into the air above Rufus but directly at him.

Miles lunged forward, "Stop! What are you doing?" The officer fired, but in the split second that Miles had distracted him, Rufus was gone.

The children were the last to know that Rufus was ever there. They had been so frightened by the gunshots and so worried about Jewel, they could think of nothing else as they urged their horses down the slippery trail. But once they saw Jewel and realized she was alive and safe, nothing else mattered. Even if Rufus had emerged and stood like a vision at the edge of the woods, they wouldn't have seen him.

Rufus, it seemed, had been forgotten. None of the officers mentioned him to Mira or Ben as they worked to tenderly free Jewel from the snare, working over her in concentrated whispers, remarking upon the damage done to her. It was as if he had never been there at all, as if they had imagined him.

Of course, in the backs of their minds, they must have remembered him and simply agreed to leave that part of the rescue out, as if it might be too hard to believe, too distracting. Another worry was this: what if the dog they had almost killed belonged to these kids? What if Miles had been right about him – that he meant no harm? What if the ranger's bullet had struck him and he was back in the woods right now bleeding to death?

Miles almost said something. He caught himself, though. He was walking with Jewel in his arms and with Mira beside him, following the other officers to their jeep while Ben followed on horseback, leading Mira's horse.

"I think God took care of her," Mira was saying. "She's so innocent and she's been through so much."

"Un huh," Miles had nodded, glancing sideways at Mira.

"Maybe he sent her a friend," he suggested tentatively, taking his time to gage her reaction, "another animal – a coyote or a wild dog to protect her."

"You think so?" Mira looked up at him.

"Well . . . it's possible. I'm just saying, you never know about these things."

Of course, he was right. In fact, Miles could not possibly have been more right, because that was the moment when Ben, riding a few yards behind Miles and hearing nothing of his conversation with Mira, was suddenly overcome by a sense of unease. He shuddered, his scalp prickling as he turned in his saddle to see Rufus looking out at him from between the trees.

CHAPTER 20

"Did you see him?" Mira was tugging at the sleeve of Ben's jacket. They were at the new house, walking side by side up the driveway, having returned the horses to the barn down the road while Jacob tended to Jewel. The officers from the ranger station had cleaned her and applied a medicated salve to the deep cuts under her shoulder but she had been frightened of them, struggling and frustrating their efforts to do a thorough job. Now, however, she was sleeping peacefully, wrapped in towels on Mira's bed.

"Did I see what?"

"Shhh . . ." They had reached the house, "I don't want Dad to hear me."

"See what, Mira?" Ben looked at his sister with the telling look of someone who knew exactly what this was about but who absolutely didn't want to discuss it.

"It was Tobias;" Mira's voice was low and steady. "I know it was. He was there, in the woods. I saw him."

"Don't be crazy. It doesn't matter what you saw." Ben turned, looking back at his sister, his hand on the door. "Tobias is dead, Mira. You need to deal with it."

"Then maybe it was his spirit. Or ... I don't know. The Ranger said there might have been another dog, a wild one, looking after her." She gave Ben the kind of fierce, desperate look she always gave him when she demanded the truth. "Just tell me. What did you see?"

Ben relaxed. He turned from the door and leaned back against it. "All right. I saw a dog." He looked at Mira, "Okay?"

"Where?"

"In the woods, on our way to the Ranger station."

"Not a coyote. A dog – right?"

Ben sighed, "I don't know, Mira. It was creepy, the way he looked at me. I thought maybe I was imagining him. And then he just melted into the woods again – just disappeared."

"Then it *was* Tobias' spirit. I'm sure of it. I saw him too, when we were lifting Jewel into the truck." Mira shivered, scanning the surrounding trees. "He looked ... young again, almost like how he used to look."

Ben studied his sister. "You know what I think?" He paused, holding her eyes, "I think it was that pup that Kwinn and his dad saw in Tacopa a few months ago. Remember? I showed them my picture of Tobias when he was young, and they said the pup they saw looked just like him."

Ben looked down; his voice was measured, "He was with his mother and the rest of her pups."

Mira drew in a breath and held it. "So you think ..." she let it out loudly, "the dog we saw was ..."

"I'm saying it could have been." Ben looked up. "I don't know. Maybe."

Mira's voice was low, almost a whisper, "And he came over 200 miles to help his sister?" She paused, "How could he do that? How would he know where to go?" Mira straightened. "He wouldn't. It was Toby, Ben; it was his spirit. That's why he appeared so mysteriously. That's why he melted away again. It was Toby."

But it wasn't, of course. It was Rufus. And he hadn't melted anywhere. He was standing, right at that moment, in the woods behind their house, invisible in the mist that had replaced the rain but very real, wet and cold and hungry. Real.

CHAPTER 21

Buckshot knew that something was up, something important. For most of the day he had been pacing back and forth ... back and forth ... while Kwinn went for more water, more supplies, talking into his cell phone as he crossed the paved lot from the Travel Center and disappearing for hours into the grove of saltbush where Bandit and Francis lay.

Buckshot was confused. First of all, he was beginning to trust Kwinn again and he wasn't sure he liked the feeling. He glanced towards the secluded circle of brush. All was quiet. Then he noticed Molly, standing alone, head down at the circle entrance. Kwinn had forgotten her too. But that wasn't the point. It was something else,

Buckshot decided that he needed to be alone. Something was expected of him but he didn't know what it was. He walked out into the desert and looked around. He decided that he would just keep walking until the answer came to him. When Friend tried to follow, Buckshot let him know with a commanding growl that he was to stay back and look after the others. Friend was part of the pack but he was not yet part of the family.

And the family was in trouble.

Evening saw Buckshot moving with a purpose. He had begun to travel north but suddenly stopped, spun around, and began going west. Buckshot was deep in concentration as he moved directly toward the setting sun …100 … 200 yards, toward where he had the strangest feeling … what was it?

Buckshot sat down. He wanted to call but something was stopping him, telling him to investigate further. Slowly he began to scent around. Who had been here? And then he knew; he could never mistake the scent of his own family. Buckshot looked up. Was this some kind of game? He looked south. No, this was serious. It was Rufus who had been here but was here no more.

Buckshot began to pace. How could Rufus have missed them? He had come so close; wouldn't he have heard the call? Then Buckshot stopped; a chill moved over him. Rufus hadn't missed them. He had heard the call but ignored it.

Buckshot began to trot, following Rufus trail. What was the matter with Rufus? His family was here; they needed him. What could be more important than that? Buckshot picked up his pace. Nothing could ever be more important than family.

Buckshot traveled thirty miles that evening, well into night. As midnight approached, he climbed a high ridge and lay down under a starless sky – vast and black with only thin wisps of cloud trailing overhead, a reminder of the storms that had come and gone. The land was dark and silent but somehow Buckshot could see clearly every rock, every shadow on the land below.

For a moment, Buckshot closed his eyes. He must be patient. If the family were to survive, he must bring Rufus home whether Rufus liked it or not. He, Buckshot, must do this – no one else.

Buckshot stood. He breathed deeply, standing tall and proud under all that sky, his eyes open, his blood surging and singing into the night. And he looked south. And he called.

Rufus heard Buckshot's call but he could not answer. It was far … far from where he stood in the forest behind the house where Jewel slept. It was farther than where he had found her today. Yet somehow it had traveled to him, honed in from a black sky over miles of majestic trees, over cool lakes and fast running streams, humming its way from the distant north.

Buckshot had found him, followed him, called from the hills where the desert began and was waiting for him to answer. Rufus felt his heart pound. It was urgent – a call for the family to reunite. But it was not a call from Bandit. Shouldn't such a call be from Bandit? Rufus remembered the truck full of bodies on the side of the highway. He had caught a faint scent of Bandit, but Bandit had not been there. What had happened to him?

Rufus stepped carefully towards the house, his heart still beating loud and insistent in his chest. He could not answer Buckshot yet – not yet, but soon.

Mira was half asleep, her body curled close to Jewel but careful not to disturb her, listening to the soft sound of her breathing, its peaceful steady cadence matching her own. A hazy light from the front of the house illumined the tall pines that lined the long drive and spread a faint glow over the dense forest beyond the corner bedroom where she lay.

If Mira had never sighed, rolled onto her back and propped her head just a bit to adjust the pillow, she would never have noticed the pair of eyes that were fixed upon her through the large circular window of beveled glass that separated her from the forest beyond.

She sat straight up, staring. But she could not see clearly through the glass. It was composed of many small slightly iridescent panes designed to permit just enough light to filter into the room, allowing the beauty of the forest to form a haunting background of deep, shimmering greens and blacks.

Mira pushed back the covers and got out of bed. She walked a few paces closer to the window and stood on tiptoe to look out of the four-inch band of pale green window-glass that surrounded the circle's translucent center. Through this glass she could see clearly. And there he was, looking down at her, his winter coat glistening in the faint light from the front of the drive.

Mira caught her breath. Ben was right. It was Jewel's brother.

For some reason, Mira was not afraid. After all, she had woken several times to the unexpected visits of Tobias, and so it seemed completely natural to put on some slippers and go outside to see what the visitor wanted.

But Rufus, true to his seemingly mystical powers, had disappeared again.

Mira stood waiting. He wasn't gone – that much she knew. After a few minutes she went inside, got a small bowl of crunchy cereal, poured some milk into it, took two graham crackers from a half empty box and carried the whole thing outside, put it down, and went back to bed.

An hour later, she awoke again. He was back. She got up, put on a sweater this time, and went outside. The crackers were gone. So why was he back? Did he want more? Did he want to see Jewel?

"I feel a little stupid, talking to nothing," she said quietly. "I know you're here. I know you saw that your sister is okay. Now," she paused, "please understand that I can't bring you into the house to see her. And I can't bring her out to see you." She sighed a long plaintive sigh, the kind that most living creatures – whatever the species, could understand. "So … what can I do? What do you want?"

The last thing Mira expected was what happened next. Rufus materialized, stood for a moment fixing her with his eyes and then turned and walked down the side of the house towards the front drive. Mira followed, mesmerized. They continued – Rufus leading, Mira following.

At the end of the drive, Rufus turned onto the road, looked over his shoulder and then stopped as if waiting for Mira. She didn't move. "I'm sorry," she whispered, remembering the last time Tobias had come to her. "I can't."

But she could. And after a few minutes in which Rufus stood patiently watching her, she said very quietly, more from her mind than from her voice, "Wait. Can you wait? Wait for me and I promise I'll follow."

CHAPTER 22

They followed on horseback shortly after 7 a.m., trying to reassure Jacob who stood unshaven in front of the house in a rumpled robe, his hair standing up in patches, displaying that unreadable worried look for which fathers are famous.

"We're going out to the lake where we found Jewel, that's all. We'll call you – okay?" with Ben looking back as he said it, trying to mirror what he hoped Jacob was thinking: *These horses are completely safe; they even know the way.* Then, adding bravely, *We really should be getting our own horses soon – not taking advantage of our neighbors like this.*

But by then they had turned the corner, still without a word from their father, loosening the reins to encourage their horses to trot while they looked back to be sure he couldn't hear them when the giggles about his appearance began.

"How do you know that's where he is, the dog you saw?" It was a few moments later.

"I just do." Mira looked at her brother, "Why do you always ask me how I know things? I don't know how; I just feel things." Then after a long pause, "I think when a person really cares a lot, I mean if you care with all your heart, it opens … like … a shortcut to what you need to know," she paused, looking away.

Mira looked back at Ben; he was starting to have that same worried look that she noticed on Jacob. "I'm not always right, Ben," she explained softly. "It's like making a good guess and being helped by your guardian angel because she knows how much it means to you."

"What about people who don't believe in angels."

Mira sighed, "That has nothing to do with it. Angels don't care if they're believed in or not." She gave her brother an exasperated look. "What's wrong with you, Ben? Angels help you because it's their job."

When Mira and Ben reached the trampled site of the snare that had held Jewel, Rufus wasn't there but Miles was. He was coming out the woods with most of his ranger gear strapped onto his back. "Hey there!" he raised his arm in greeting, sliding down through the undergrowth to meet them. "Good to see you!" He stopped, "How's she doing?"

"She's good," Mira smiled, "much better!"

Miles nodded. He seemed uncertain about something. Mira studied him.

"We're looking for her brother," she said suddenly. "He followed us home but then he disappeared. Have you seen him?"

Miles was obviously relieved. "No, not today. I hoped he wasn't – you know, hurt yesterday." He looked away as if embarrassed. "I've got some triage supplies here, been searching for him all morning." He stopped, looking up at Mira, "So when you saw him, he was okay?"

Mira nodded; she smiled again, "He's good, but thanks for caring about him." She sighed, scanning the woods behind Miles and then turning to Ben, "Guess we need to look somewhere else."

But then, just as the two turned away because it certainly seemed that wherever Rufus was, he wasn't there, Miles startled them with "Wait! He *is* here. Look!"

And there he was, magical Rufus, standing on top of the slope above them, his thick reddish coat shining gold where a shaft of sunlight struck it from between a cluster of young pines that spread a canopy of branches over him.

They followed him all day, through the hills, under the highway, through more hills and then finally out onto the desert heading north. By early afternoon, they were traveling parallel to a lone two-lane blacktop that thankfully presented a route sign.

Ben texted Jacob, described their location and promised to contact him soon again. Like Mira, he had no idea where Rufus was leading them, but also like Mira he had resigned himself to this trip, trusting that this son of Tobias, this almost exact duplicate of Tobias, who loved his sister so much he had risked his life to find her, would not let them down.

And he didn't. His reunion with Buckshot was a sight that neither Ben nor Mira would ever forget. It was late afternoon; the desert floor a cool stretch of indigo – blues and greys, long trails of light and shadow that led to the horizon.

Then, in the distance, a single streak of dusty iron bronze. Rufus saw it first; he stopped, frozen, the skin beneath his fur rippling with excitement. Mira and Ben moved up beside him, their eyes fixed on the same image. For a few moments no one moved; no one spoke.

And then, coming out of nowhere, the long loping form of Buckshot, his joy at seeing his brother leaving Ben and Mira in awe, the kind of rapt wonder for which no words can do justice.

And so as twilight's regal mantle spread slowly across the darkening desert, they allowed Buckshot to lead them. Later, when twilight deepened into dusk, Rufus moved up beside Buckshot, and the brothers trotted side by side to lead Mira and Ben the final mile to the campsite where Bandit lay.

When Mira first saw Kwinn, kneeling beside his father who was treating the motionless form of Bandit beside their small fire, her heart thumped. She never expected to see him out here, so far from the little store where they first had met. It was at his campsite that she and Ben had learned for the first time that Tobias' pups existed.

She had seen him once again, but as in their first meeting he had disappeared without a word, picking her up when she was lost and half asleep, taking her on his horse to Tobias' grave, sliding her down gently. He had paused, giving her the softest look, but then … he was gone.

Both meetings had been dreamlike, so that looking back she had wondered how real Kwinn actually was. But now, in the firelight beside Bandit, shielding his eyes as he rose to greet her, her fears dissolved. Of course he was real. And he was here!

"Hi," she said softly. Kwinn smiled. He took her hand and immediately Mira relaxed.

"My father," he said as they walked to the fire, "do you remember?"

Mira nodded. How could she ever forget that night at their campsite along the Amargosa River Trail. "He told us that the pup he saw was too young to be Tobias, but that he would be safe."

Mira looked across the fire to where Rufus stood gazing at his unmoving brother. Kwinn followed her gaze, just as his father looked up also and saw Rufus.

"He found us," Mira whispered. "He found his sister and then he brought us here."

"Father Bernardo has blessed him," Kwinn crouched down beside his father. He looked up at Mira and smiled. "He hid beneath the chapel; that's where he stayed to hide his grief, after his mother was killed."

"And now he's here with ..." Mira's voice trailed off.

"Yes, with his dying brother, with all of his brothers."

Ben, who had been holding the reins for both horses, let them drop. He approached the fire and knelt next to Kwinn's father, "Was he," he looked at Bandit, "also coming for his sister when ... "

"Yes," Kwinn's father pressed gently on the gauze pad over Bandit's heart. "At dawn I will take him up to Big Pine where he will sleep with his ancestors. But he is very weak, maybe too weak to ride in the truck. We will see ... at dawn."

Ben stood suddenly, startling the little group around the fire. Buckshot and Friend jumped up. "He needs Jewel," Ben looked down at Mira and Kwinn. "He needs to see her now ... soon."

"That's right," Mira stood and moved over to Ben. "We took her from him; now we need to bring her back to him."

Kwinn stood, "Yes. It would be good for him to see her. Father … ?"

Kwinn's father looked up. He nodded slowly, returning his attention to Bandit as Mira dug in her pocket for her phone. She glanced at Kwinn who directed her and Ben to " the second pole light – there on the paved lot."

They walked fast; everything seemed to be moving quickly now. Jacob said yes, of course he would bring Jewel; he would make her a bed next to him in the front of the pickup. He could locate the Travel Plaza easily, he told Ben. No problem – just give him a few hours.

Mira's heart was beating a new kind of beat as they returned to the fire – the kind of beat that is a relief, a lightness, the reward for doing what one knows without a doubt is the right thing to do.

And of course the smile, the warmth in Kwinn's eyes as she sat beside him, was a feeling she never knew she longed for all her life.

CHAPTER 23

It was midnight when Jewel arrived. Bandit was still alive, slipping in and out of consciousness, occasionally lifting his head to look around before sighing painfully and sinking down again.

"His soul is strong; he has great courage." Kwinn's father sat back, admiring Bandit. He and Kwinn had been tending to Bandit's wounds while Buckshot and Rufus lay close by. Francis, whose stomach was tightly wrapped and whose neck where a second bullet had torn the flesh was just beginning to heal, lay between them.

As everyone watched, Jacob carried Jewel wrapped in a blanket to Bandit's side. No one moved. No canine jumped to defend. No human stood or spoke. The world was still.

Jewel, once Jacob put her down and backed away, struggled to lift herself into a position where she could see Bandit. She pushed closer. She sniffed at him; she licked his face.

Bandit opened his eyes. He tried to greet her but she stopped him, moving up to his mouth, kissing it, her breath on his so that he could feel her life and feel that she was giving it to him.

Bandit sighed. His heartbeat slowed. Now he could sleep. He had found his sister.

It was as if the quieting of Bandit's heart, the slow rhythmic beat that now replaced the irregular stop/start/stop which had endangered his life, spread its message through the night air and laid its peace upon the little group. Kwinn's father and Jacob spoke quietly. Ben lay close to the horses, closing his eyes and never noticing when Francis crept up beside him and sighed with contentment.

Kwinn, as usual, spoke little with words, but when he gently touched Mira's hair and then her face, and offered his shoulder for her nodding head to rest upon, no words were needed.

It was several hours before dawn when Mira opened her eyes. Across the firelight she could see Rufus. He stood so still, so perfect, his bronze coat streaked with gold from the light of the fire, his large intense eyes shadowed so that she barely glimpsed their question.

He looks so much like Tobias, she was thinking, *the way he looked the night he came to say goodbye.* She had often wondered if Tobias had been real that night, or just a vision, just a dream. But Rufus was real. And he was talking to her with his eyes.

Mira smiled. *Yes,* she said without words, because whatever he wanted she trusted it to be good. Slowly Rufus approached Jewel from the other side of where she lay against Bandit. He kissed her and then he lay down against her. Mira's eyes filled. She glanced up to see if Kwinn was watching. He was.

If Mira could have composed a prayer to say thank you

for the gift of seeing such a moment, she would have done so. But she couldn't. Maybe there are times when the sense of awe we creatures feel when gazing upon something so naturally beautiful is enough – is prayer enough.

Early the next morning as Kwinn's father was preparing to leave, sharing a coffee with Jacob, wrapping his supplies and then working to create a space for Bandit in the bed of his truck, Mira surprised them both by approaching them bravely and stating the decision she had made with Kwinn just as dawn was breaking.

"I'm going to Big Pine with Jewel, Dad. We'll ride in the back with Bandit so he can feel her close to him." She glanced at Kwinn's father, "If it's okay with you." She took a breath.

Everyone stopped what they were doing, eyes glued to Mira.

She turned back to Jacob, "I'm friends with Kwinn's sister, Dad. We camped together on the trail that night in Tacopa." Mira took another breath. "Kwinn called his mom and she said yes, I'm welcome to stay with them."

She paused, glancing at Ben and Kwinn for support, "Bandit shouldn't lose Jewel so soon. He just found her, so I hope you'll say yes. Okay?"

Jacob sighed. What could he do? There was no refusing Mira at a time like this. "Call me," he said simply, "and be good."

It was still early morning. Mira, Jewel, and Bandit were settled securely in the bed of Kwinn's father's pick-up when at the last moment, just they were beginning to pull away, Rufus leaped into the back of the truck to join them. He ignored Mira and padded right up to Bandit, checked him out, and then moved to where Jewel lay beside him, making a bed for himself beside her on her pile of blankets. He looked up at Mira as if to say, "See? Here I am again," and then lay down with a satisfied thump.

Kwinn, who had mounted Molly and was watching, laughed. "Father Bernardo will be glad to see you, Rufus. He's up in Big Pine – right where you're going."

Kwinn took Francis from Ben and secured him on his lap. He turned Molly to begin their long ride back to Tacopa. Buckshot moved to his one side and Friend to the other. "Be safe," Mira called.

"Oh, I'm sure we're safe enough," Kwinn laughed again.

As they took off, the two canines trotted out in front. Mira watched in amazement as Friend moved instinctively to the right of Buckshot, shoulder to shoulder. "His left eye can be Buckshot's right eye," Kwinn had explained to her the night before. "I've seen them practice. Buckshot probably won't need it," he added, "but just in case."

Kwinn turned and paused. He called to Mira, "I'll be in Big Pine in a few days. Maybe I'll see you."

"Okay, maybe," Mira called softly, turning her head with a sly smile.

"Thanks, Dad. Thanks, Ben." She called, watching them prepare to head back home with the two horses in tow, " I love you."

It was evening when Kwinn arrived at Ella's porch with Francis. "Here's your little hero," he said with a smile. "Take care of him."

He watched as she and Paul took Francis carefully from him and brought him inside, with Paul holding the door for Ella and giving Kwinn a grateful look.

It was a beautiful night, a good night; all was well in God's desert, in the hearts of men and in the hearts of His creatures far and wide as in the distance, across the mountains, God's own dogs, his beloved coyotes, lifted up their ancient song of praise and Kwinn, Buckshot and Friend, secure in that song, headed for Big Pine.

Finis

BOOKS BY BOBBI BOLAND WHITE

ESCAPE FROM MARIANNA, available in print and digital. Young Adult award-winner. 2011. Kirkus review, 2017.

THE TOBIAS TRILOGY:
Recommended: Teen through Adult

A PRAYER FOR TOBIAS, Available in print and digital – mid 2017.

TOBIAS RETURNS: A CALL FOR HELP. Available in print and digital – mid 2017.

THE SONS OF TOBIAS, Available in print and digital – winter, 2017.

Author information: Bobbi Boland White,
AMAZON: amazon.com/author/Bobbi Boland White
FACEBOOK: BobbiBolandWhite – BBWhite (email me)
TWITTER: Bobbi.White, BBWhite @bbwmanagement
bbwmanagement@aol.com
bobbi.white1@aol.com